The Chronicles of Lord River Part 2

Billy Michaells Thceascza

Library of Congress Control Number:		2014902347
ISBN:	Hardcover	978-1-4931-7170-5
	Softcover	978-1-4931-7169-9
	eBook	978-1-4931-7171-2

This book was printed in the United States of America.

Rev. date: 02/03/2014

To order additional copies of this book, contact:
Xlibris LLC
1-888-795-4274
www.Xlibris.com
Orders@Xlibris.com
540467

CONTENTS

Easter, Guy of Halloween, and the Time Machinc Man of Holiday

The Town Who Forgot about Christmas!

Toolip and Airlie The Quest for Paradise

By Joseph Mickey Lluvera

Hello, readers! I have a treat from me to you. A present from Santa Claus. This one is called "Easter, Guy of Halloween, and the Time Machine Man of Holiday." After, you can read a great short story called "The Town Who Forgot about Christmas." And third, I have a beautiful treat called "Toolip and Airlie!" So sit back and enjoy this hard-core epic of Santa's struggle in his new world, Holiday, and a critical event Santa had to go through. Plus, there is a father and son's quest for pure power to bring their world into paradise. Read and you will enjoy.

Easter, Guy of Halloween, and the Time Machine Man of Holiday

1

A Beautiful Day!

IT WAS A beautiful day. Crowds are out looking at the man in the red suit who is about to change history. Mr. Chris Cringle had built his greatest project yet . . . a time machine. Out of all the inventions and toys he and his lovely wife, Mrs. Sandy Cringle, have made, this one was the best. He made action figures and dolls for the children; he also invented cars and machinery. He then made a project for airplanes. The year is 1940 in New York City, Earth. Life is sweet for everyone and it keeps getting better. In the newspapers his name rang bells. His picture is everywhere. Now he had built a time machine! In the back of the stage, stage left, with his wife, she preps him like always.

"Okay, Chris, listen to my words now." His heart's pounding and his face sweating a little. "This is the time you prove to the world what really you are. Now it's your world, and all other worlds will want some of it. So just go out there and get all of it . . ." She giggles a little and then kisses him. "It's all yours now. Make it happen, dear."

"Okay. Okay, Sandy. I'll be ready in a second." Chris faints on the floor. Some people come to his aid backstage.

On the stage with the new and improved time machine under a red sheet, people speculate about how it looks. It's outside and anyone can see it. He's finally up now, and he's now ready to tell the world what he had accomplished. He as a human had made a toy that can travel in time. In color holes. Holes that go to other worlds and with other types of ozone colors too. They have different day and nighttimes there. His floating aircraft is mainly made to drive to other destinations. He's traveled to two worlds so far. And he is going to one of them again today in front of everyone. The one where he can give the parents of the best part he see fit and give them gifts. He goes all over their world in just one day. He's now going to tell it to New York City and all who watch television.

An announcer comes out on stage and begins to speak . . . "Ladies and gentlemen! I am here to bring to you the most creative man alive! The man of the year. The best inventor there is on the face of Earth. Here for you today . . . Mr. Chris Cringle!" He comes out on stage a little paranoid.

"People of the world! I'm here for you to give other worlds what we have!" The crowd looks on in anticipation. He looks on and talks as he pulls the cover off of his greatest machine. "And if it can take me anywhere, imagine the possibilities!" Everyone sees the floating machine just in thin air on the outside stage. They clapped. And cheered on. He smiled off the ears from the cheeks.

"Hey, Mr. Cringle. Show us how it works?"

"Sure, in just a second. I want to say a few words. I will go off to a faraway land. I world even for my new invention will take me there without a shadow of a doubt. It's my flying time portal machine . . . *the Clause*!" It was a wonderful thing like as if it was alive.

All red with white lining around it. Ice skates on the bottom of it. A big bag of toys and things for grown-ups also in the back of it. It too was red. Like a cloth but elastic. It was filled to the brim. And still more on the sleigh desk where Chris sits in front of. With five extra sleigh desks chained with five other bags in them. It was enough to fill up the whole block of Twenty-Third Street. At three o'clock, Tuesday, June 20, 1940, he was about to do the inevitable. "This machine called the Clause will take me to the place and time I would want to go to. And these toys are for the people I observed for two years now in just two trips. And some will gain all of our stuff and some will have to work better to get it later. But all will know of the Santa Clause of the Clause—me! In just a minute I will enter this craft and an invisible bubble will cover me. And I will teleport into the best known hole I want. In this world people are like you and me. Two-armed and two-legged, one-headed creatures that love to help their fellow world as I do. These are their pictures . . ." He showed them pictures of extraterrestrials. "Living in huts made of brick and stone from their surface. Not so advanced. But they're very happy.

"They will see me not as their huts change with my inventions I will give them. I will leave in five minutes! And I will return in an hour. Fulfilled from my job. Then soon I will train some of you people to help me along the travels in the future. Primitive people we are not. And we will help all in our own way." He goes off to the backstage left to suit up. His wife helps him. "Now, Chris, it's almost over. All you have to do is show them what you got. You can't fail us now."

"Fail us? What if I wake up some people and they catch me and eat me or something. I don't know. All I know is I have some fine knitted furniture and toys for them, and I pray that they do not see me."

"Don't worry yourself, Chris. I mean, come on, you have all your life ahead of you. Besides . . . if you get killed, I'll travel back in time and kill them before they kill you, so let's get it moving. Put your hat on. It looks comfy on you."

"Okay, Sandy. I'll make sure you keep in touch with me by never stop talking to you over the c.d. and you . . ."

"Won't stop talking to you either, Chris. I love you. Turn on the right buttons before you teleport."

"Sure thing, honey." He goes in front of the large crowd looking at him with his beautiful suit on. All was amazed at the fact that he was saying all of this stuff and is actually going to do such a job.

He gets into the floating machine but places the gadgets in his suit first. Then it just lit up like Christmas lights across his sleigh. The bubble shines in sections around the top of the sleigh. It quickly shot up into the sky and then disappeared. As he appeared in the deep space he looks around playing with some buttons, typing things down and pulling some panels. Then out of the blue a blue hole appeared. "That's correct data?"

He spoke to his wife. "No, it's not the same whole print."

"Okay. How are we doing on Earth?"

"Fine, honey. Did it come yet?"

"No. But I have a feeling it will in five more seconds."

Then another black hole in the blue color appeared. The speaking database spoke . . . "Correct prints upon finding."

"Good data! Good! Okay. Three hundred and four, here we come." He pushes the panel down and then presses a button that shoots him straight into the blue hole.

On the other side, Chris shot out of the blue hole into a blue ozone layer like Earth's, but it was a triangle shape and not a round shape. Inside of the ozone layer he shoots down in an invisible bubble around the whole sleigh floating in the air. It floats on top of a hut.

"Ah, Tummie's house." He goes in the house to check up on them. "Sound asleep." He goes out and places two soft cotton beds and dressers for themselves outside of their house. Plus the toys for the children.

He did this to every house all over that world where people lived at on that planet in just one night. Teleporting in front of each house. Placing their stuff outside their huts. Then jetting off. At the last house that same night he finished in an exhausting happiness. "A job well done. I came here at three forty-five and it's now two days done passed. I teleported for the stuff for them back and forth home to new world for me, almost broke the time machine down, and look at here . . . It's only 3:53 a.m., just eight minutes done passed, wonderful, right, Sandy?"

"Sure thing. Now come on home, Chris. I'm lonely."

"It's only been an hour there, Sandy."

"But still, Chris, come home, okay? It could be dangerous out there, you know."

"Now you tell me." He laughs. Then shoots off back to Earth.

Meanwhile in a far-out world where the ozone layer is a bright pink, there lived the first world of the holidays all on one planet. Their leader and beautiful mother, Easter, came from a world where Bunnies ruled with April Fool's Kids and life was very fast there although they lived for such a short time they come to this world called Holiday! All of the other holiday people lived there with them. Four presidents. Lincoln, George, Benjamin, and Adam. The guys and girls are of Halloween. They too look extraterrestrial but they are scary looking. The first ones on Holiday. The Thanksgiving turkeys, two gray turkeys with a family of a male turkeys with them. Father's Day is for Rabbit Bunny from Easter's family. And there just about twenty Bunnies there.

And also the color holes for the Fourth of July lights. They will bring Chris to their world for Easter and Rabbit. They watched him help that entire world, and it influenced them to do the same. Also on that planet were the Labor Day teachers and Principal O'Connell, the best teacher in a world like Earth. Cupids from the yellow worlds. The oldest they look is at about five years old. They have wings and they fly. They have the wooden soldiers for March. They create all types of marches for all to watch. The New Year infants, they too never get old. Always in a baby carriage. The Memorial Day soldiers of wars are there too.

They are amazed how he can make all of those inventions and how he can alter time like that and still keep the laws of time together. "It was harmless, Easter. I would have thought it would break the hole in pieces."

"Imagine him helping us with our dreams. If we can get him here it would be special blue light leader."

"I'll do my best, Easter." Rabbit was there also. He said, "And blue light leader, try not to hurt him. Let him think he just appeared here on his own."

"Yes . . . Rabbit, we will do our best."

"Thank you, Blue Light."

As Easter sat on her throne with Rabbit sitting beside her. Their palace was beautiful. Pearly snow white and shiny. With rainbow colors alongside the walls and roofs. Inside had fourteen rooms on four floors of them all. Bunnies lived all in them. Bigga Bunny and Bugsy Bunny were the oldest. They trained with the April Fool's Kids in the trickiest ways. The two Bunnies always prevailed.

As they look on to Chris going back home. They think of how they will convince him to live with them on their world to help the people. Soon they must make one. "Oh, I have a plan!" Rabbit Bunny spoke out loud. Their ear listens in and reads all he is saying.

"Guy and girl definitely want in on this one." They get a little frantic. "Come on, Bunnies. It'll prove how strong he truly is. We must kill him to keep him on our world." Rabbit said, "No! That would not be good. We can wait for his death. And his wife . . . it is not a good idea."

"But, Easter . . . for your first child."

"No! It is final."

Rabbit then said, "Okay. But how will he be a part of our world?"

"By letting him live his life. He will love it here once he is born on Holiday. Just be patient!"

As they speak Chris is now home from a long trip of five minutes in their earthly time. "Life is just ten times better. I can't believe it." They cheer on louder than anything before. All for Chris, his wife, and his Clause.

"Honey. This is the beginning of a beautiful relationship."

"With you! I thought . . ."

"No, silly, I mean . . . with them." They look on as they all cheer for him.

At his office in Long Island. A huge two floor building where short children are hired to make the toys. Plus, they create the equipment for the machines that make the grown-up stuff for him two blocks down. He pays them good. They support their family the most these days. "Put the circuits over there. I'll look at them later. Honey! I was looking at some days to have this occasion for Earth. How about on December 25? And we'll call it Christmas Day. I'll place all the toys and high-tech stuff here. On Christmas. On the earth. How's that?"

"That's good, dear. I love it."

"Good?"

"Good."

"Here, I got it all written down."

"Oh, I see . . . a tree in the house with beautiful ornaments on them. All in my name. For Mrs. Clause is the shining light on the top of the tree."

"That's wonderful, dear. Thank you."

"You're welcome, honey. Oh no, put that over there. That's for the winding dolls and the hula hoops. Honey . . . did anything break?"

"Just those vases for the flower."

"Oh, how many?"

"Just about five of them."

"Dope!"

"Honey . . . I got to go on another trip. I found a hole last night. It was pink. On the screen I checked it. It looks very harmless. I want to go there in three days. Is it okay?"

"Sure thing, baby boy. Just don't get hurt or anything. I'll be safe for you here. Be safe for me there."

"You got it."

That day he was all packed up. With just the machine, not any sleigh carts filled with inventions or toys. He looks at everything and checks it. "And sleigh hallow screen good, check." He gets the suit on with his wife's help. It's light, but he still needs help from his wonderful wife.

"Okay, honey, all is well on this side."

"Yes! All is well here also. Prepare the fire shooters." The machine floats up a little the ladder shoots out. He climbs in and turns it on for the lights to shine out.

"I'll see you in a little while, honey."

"Okay. Keep in touch with me at all times, Chris." He opens up the garage door, gets in his Clause, turns it on full power, and flies out into the night sky. He shoots up into the night space to catch the same pink hole to see what's on the other side.

Going to the same spot as last night, he waits for it to appear. On five minutes going by. He sees it in the far corner of his Clause. He catches the correct analysis. "It's the one. Let's go, Clause, we have much work to do." And he shoots inside of the pink hole. As he shoot's out of it he drops into the pink ozone layer. He loses contact with his wife.

"Sandy! Come in! Sandy!" The color of the ozone pulls him down on to the atmosphere. "Oh my god, something's pulling me down!" He screams off the top of his lungs until the light drops him off on the surface. After a while he got control of the spacecraft. He moved along in the invisible light around it. No one could see him or the spacecraft. He tries to stay hidden from any creature on that planet. He landed on plain ground.

"Looks like no one's here yet. Let's look around some more. Maybe I'll find some life here like it said there was." He traveled and nowhere was anyone. He flew around until he found some life. It was odd for they looked like two tiny extraterrestrials, the two of them. One female watching one larger male be chased down by a huge dinosaur. It looks like with one more step he was about to be squashed. She cries in paranoia for him until the huge dinosaur stomped on him with ease. She cries, and Chris cries for dear life for a few as the dinosaur walked away they saw the bloody remains of the male.

The two in his spacecraft and her on the ground. But out of nowhere the same male appears like his teleport craft does. He walks up to her and scares the hell out of her. "But you were just dead!" She cries and pulls out an ax. "I'm a kill you for that!" She chops off his hand. Chris sees all the blood and faints in the spacecraft.

2

Where's my Clause?

AT EASTER'S PALACE they laugh at how Chris faints. "He is surely a strong one, Rabbit."

"Wait until he sees what else is in store for him, Mother."

"I'm sure I can't wait, Rabbit." As Chris wakes up he notices that he's out of his time machine and on the forest ground. Startled, he gets up and yells but shuts up in fear.

"Where in God's name am I?"

"You're in our first world from all other worlds including the earth. It is called the Holiday!"

"What is this about? I mean am I going to be trailed for trespassing or something."

"No . . . we need your help. Are you willing to accept?"

"Yes. I mean, I mean it all depends. Is it a life-threatening type of help where I make a wish or I die or is it nice and exciting."

"It is not about death for you, but you will surely die."

"Tonight you will have to save a kid. It will be your most dangerous task. He is held captive by a bunch of army soldiers. You must rescue him before the ransom is paid."

"And how do I do that? Like with my time machine or something?"

"Correct-o mondo!"

"Who are you? Where are you, and where am I?"

"I'm the kid you have to rescue."

"But if you're the kid . . . Hey!" The April Fool's kid laughs off as Chris tries to get up from the red soil. One of the three Kids said, "I'm Apo, this is Tomo, and he's Yomo. And we are some of the April Fool's Kids. Yeah, we don't play yo!" He looks around. The same purple mint trees and large bush trees, so bushy a bunch of people can live in it. Of course a bunch does. And in the trees are soldiers. They secretly look at the Kids and Chris Cringle.

The Memorial Day soldiers were camping out and saw the time machine. They grabbed it up for themselves. You can see them in their camouflage and equipment. The Clause with them tied up by the trees vines they made. Chris looks up and is startled to see them. "What the . . . who are you things?"

"We lived on the earth also, maggot. Just like those Kids you're with. Now who are you?" one of the soldiers said to Chris.

"Well, I'm Chris. Chris Cringle from New York City."

"Of course you live in Yankees Ville. A pussy clot like those in the Caribbean says in the 1990s," Tomo said to Chris.

He replied, "Huh . . . I don't understand."

"Of course you don't woo you just got here. Plus, you came here without dying, not like the rest of us. Now that was sweet," Tomo said.

Yomo says while squeezing his skin, "He's soft, Apo. Can we keep him?"

A soldier said in the trees, "Now, Private, you just can't go picking up stray creatures these days. It just can kill you. Instantly, I mean like *pow*, right in the kisser." Apo then said, "So, Chris. Happy trails, go home, I had a nice time. Wherever you came from, go back. See yaw later, alligator. Well, you're not an alligator, you too soft swine food!"

Chris said, "What if I tell you I can give you a gift you will love? It's nothing you ever saw before. It's from my time and I made one. If you just would give me my time machine. I can make it all better for all of us."

The soldier said, "Time machine! What time machine? I never heard of nothing like that. Besides, ain't that stuff like that fake or something. I don't know, maggot. Anyway, I told you it'll be worth your while," Chris said, looking up at the trees, not noticing his time machine there.

"Oh, you must be talking about that thing you were sleeping in earlier. Well, I got it right here. In the bushes with me, see?" It was high up there. He almost fainted to think it would fall out of the bush tree.

"Well, Chris! I think you better just run along now before my soldiers get a little frisky."

"No! Not without my time machine!" He yells out so loud the tree vibrated. The soldiers began aiming at him with their rifles.

Three said, "Hold still, maggot!"

In fear, Chris said, "Okay! Okay!" He said it while holding his hands up. He stands still. "If you move one more time, maggot, we will fire you a new hole between your legs." The April Fool's Kids ran behind Chris. Apo said, "They fin to kill us finally we dead we all dead. Remember, Guy wants to kill him anyway. Maybe he wants us dead too or something." Chris overheard that.

He said, "Kill me. What?"

Tomo said, "Yeah, Chris, you saw Guy's kids outside playing without his permission. One died twice that night . . ." The soldiers then put their rifles down and stood firm.

Apo then said, "Yeah, one by that huge Tyrannosaurus and one by his sister. Her seeing something like that for the first time startled her. But she's all right like you are as I can see until it happens to you!" The sergeant waves his hand; the soldiers retreat in the bushes.

A voice of the sergeants spoke out. "Move out, maggots. Let's go! Let's go! This here is mine now." He laughs, talking about the Clause. Chris stands there without anything to help him in the forest.

One of the April Fool's Kids said, "Oh, they heading toward No Where Ends. That's cool. Come on, let's go before Mom gets at us." They leave off into the forest. With many paths in front of him to No Where Ends on the end of them.

"Who wants to take a trip to No Where Ends?" Chris said.

"The sign says it's right square splat. I wonder if I'll be all right." He looks behind him and sees another road. "Short Road Ends. That's interesting." Now he has two choices. Let's hope it's the right one.

As he look at both roads, No Where Ends and Short Road Ends, one looks straight and the other has four different roads. No Where Ends was the road with he suggest to . . . "I might as well go on one of the two roads because I see one of them ending up straight far where those soldiers went with my Clause. But this one does not. So I will not choose this one. But why do they want me to move for, they took my time machine and left north. Under No Where Ends Road. Where did they go on top of the tree bushes? I don't know, but I will find out. And why."

As he began to walk toward No Where Ends Road, a groundhog the size of a dog trembled the red soil earth, making Chris fall. He pops out of the forest ground, saying, "Fee-fi-fo-fum, I smell the skin of an Englishman! What do you know of the Holiday? Our world is far too true for you . . . Umm you're pure flesh. I smell it on you. Fully alive!"

"I would hope so," Chris replied. He gets up from the ground and tries to run the straight road in fear he'll speed away.

"Wait a sec, chap! I still ain't got your name . . ." He then jumps up and into the ground, chasing after him. As he passes him he then jumps out of the ground, stopping him.

"Hey, big fellow, easy. I never saw a groundhog so huge!"

"Groundhog I am. My names Cheerios. And yours?"

"Chris."

"Just sit tight, chap. I have some good news for you. If you go down the road that you're on you will find the mother of our world, and she will give you things you never saw before. But there's just one thing . . ." He crawls up to him quickly and says, "You have to fight Guy of Halloween in a duel to the death today your toy against him. That's the only way you can return harmless. He saw you this morning looking at him kill his poor young son as a dinosaur. Again, Girl . . ."

"I'm not a girl . . ."

"No, that's her name—Girl! Chap! Keep up with me I ain't going so fast now, ain't I? Now he wants to kill you a couple of times and he said . . ."

"Wait a minute, a couple of times? Where am I? In hell or something?" He began hyperventilating and sweating. Talking to himself alone pardoning his back to Cheerios. "This can't be seriously sane for me. I'm a . . . I'm an American for Christ's sake on Earth. And what I feel pain or something then I'll be all fuck—"

He's interrupted by Cheerios. "Hey, Chris, quiet down over there. Don't worry, you're not going to feel no pain. Luckily for you, our day has twenty-two hours in it so you have enough time to find Captain Hopkins. He has your time machine with him. You get it from him you might have a chance to fight him off. You know Guy. Guy of Halloween? But anyway . . ."

"If I get my time machine I could kill him first . . . ," Chris whispers to himself. "Or I can just fly my way out of here. Back home, you know, the easy way out of it. I can be back with my wife and everything. Oh, I know she's worried."

"I don't know about that, Chris," Cheerios said, listening in on Chris's conversation with himself. "See they couldn't figure out the buttons and things, chap, so they broke it a little. It's going to take a little time for you to fix it, so you will still have to be here to kill him, chap."

He quickly turns around. "Look here, chap or whatever, I don't have time to be killing anyone. I just want my machine back so I can leave. Look, I just started this, and I will automatically stop it if you would just let me go home!"

"See, chap . . . that could have been the case, but you saw him kill his son then his sister chopped his son's arm up. That's self-mutilation, plus attempted murder, and you're the witness."

"And what are you? The messenger?"

"Sure thing, I do not want to die tonight by that Halloween might . . ."

"I don't know what to do . . ."

He starts to cry. Cheerios looked at him in sympathy. "But I have a suggestion. If you go down this road now, you can find Hopkins early, and after, you can go off to see the mother. Mother Easter, that is. She maybe can stop the fight or whatever it is and go home! Now does that sound like a good idea?"

"Of course it does!" His eyes lit up like candles as he wanted to rush down that road to find Hopkins. "If I find Captain Hopkins I'll be fine then. Is that what you're saying?"

"Yes, old chap, it is. Now hurry, Chris, you don't have the time to waste."

He began to run down the road up until he saw the same-looking four roads as the other road.

"What in God's name is this? It's just like the other road." He stands their as if he's deciding which road to choose. As he looked on he thought a little and then said, "Now let me see . . . I believe that each road ends up in the same direction! So choose any of the four roads." He goes off to find Hopkins for his time machine.

"See ya later, have fun, and beware of the golden leprechauns—they love to eat human flesh."

Chris turns around in fear. "What kind of place is this? I truly have to get out of here, pronto."

As Easter looks on in her pearly white palace, in front of the sheet screen where they all watch Chris in the forest. She laughs in fun about what's happening to young Chris. "Ha, he's worth it. Look at him so patient, so nice."

Rabbit then said, "And so freaking paranoid. Look at him. Eyes coming out of his head."

Easter replies, "Look here, my first child and most favorite with Bugsy Bunny. I hope you're watching without any feelings. He will be the one to help us all. That time machine is remarkable. It can connect all the worlds one behind the other. It is not my fault that he is going to be the ruler of us above me."

"Funny how your still saying that, Mother Easter. What if it gets out in the open, Chris there would become chowder for our dinner."

"It's already out there and all agree to this," Easter said.

Rabbit then said, "Then I agree as well. But we did agree that my nominee, the Wonka, had better ties you'll see."

"Wonka did not succeed in his health goal. Now Chris will be our Clause. He can even make his toys become real now through us."

Just right outside of the palace, Bugsy and Bigga just fell in a trapped ditch a little deep in the ground. It was made by Ak, To, and Peepee of the April Fool's Kids. They are always fighting each other, for they both love carrots, and there are not a lot of carrots being grown in their gardens yet. Ak and the three laugh. "So you stupid bunnies still think you smarter than us, huh? Now where's our carrots!"

Bugsy said, "Of course we will not tell you, but for your carrots in the stash can get me to talk."

Bigga then said, "Oh yeah. Watch this!" He hops right out of the ditch and kicks Peepee in the face. "You bet I'm smarter than all of you."

"Yeah. And how's that?" To said, moving out of the way with Ak. But then Bugsy jumps out also and kicks the both of them in their faces. They fall.

"Come on, you three. We got to go to school. Before Mr. O'Connell expels you three," Bigga said, laughing.

Ak said, "Yeah, we'll be there before you two nerds. Their bullying does not make them intelligent in any way. What losers, right big brother?" Bugsy says walking off to school. Bigga replied, "Yeah, they are not in-terligent . . . or something."

"Bigga Bunny. The proper expression is 'intelligent,' okay?"

"Sure thing! Little Bunny. Let's go, we're going to be late!" They go hopping away.

And Goon, Guy's son, is out in the oak tree forest. Looking at the dinosaur. With just a beam of light the giant dinosaur disappeared. And on the plain outside of the oak tree forest where Goon is watching the other Halloween come jogging toward Goon. He's the father of Halloween. He's Guy! <image 3: Two alien or extraterrestrials looking as evil laughing at their female family member they just scared to death.> All Halloweens look like two-legged debarment. So Guy and his son, Goon, looked almost the same, but they can change into any creature. Plus, they have resurrection abilities. Guy said to Goon in a deep voice, "Did your sister cast you out or love the magic trick?"

"She loved it later on but vowed to get revenge on me."

"I know just what family to place her in. You know we can tell a Halloween from a mile away. But if there's bunches of the same creatures we seem to not choose the correct one, but we still would have the best advantage."

"Yes, Father. We 'rectum' Halloweens are the first Halloweens ever."

"True indeed, my child. Now let's go to Mother. She might have some of our favorite pig sauce and rice for tonight."

"True, Father. I hope my poor dear sister is home already. I don't know what Mother would do to her for being late for supper."

"She may scold her to death. And did you see our new friend watching on today when you stomped your son out?"

"Why, yes, I did. He fainted all over his airplane thingie. Are you going to kill him?"

"I will. Only because he can fly in that tin. So I'll have to scare him to death."

"Good idea, Father. Let's go home. I'm so hungry I can eat a horse!" Echoes sound out in the trees from his voice.

In school, the auditorium was packed. All different kinds of children are there. A lot more Bunnies, Kids, even Halloweeners and Kupids. The children of the president were there. Mr. O'Connell is in front of his students on stage behind a mantle and microphone ready to speak to them. Everyone's quickly getting quiet as the principal looks on. They are quiet now. He says, "My fellow students! We now have a goal for us to succeed in. A goal that will hype up all of the future of our world. Holiday! Life will become better right before our eyes. There is a new comer to our world. He is the most successful of us all. His name will be . . . The Santa Clause of Christmas!" The students talk a little about it.

Then Bugsy says, "This must be that man not dead here from Earth Mother was talking about, right, Bigga?"

"I think so, Bugs, I think so. I didn't think it was going to get this deep. He's talked about all in here now."

"Yeah. That's some deep straddles."

Mr. O'Connell speaks a little more. "Yes, my children, calm down and listen. He's an inventor. He invents things for all of the worlds. And we will help him succeed. You elves over there, you love to work. You come from Labor Day. You can do anything. So you will be his helpers. We have it all planed out for all of us to enjoy. We will be the greatest world ever with him! And Christmas will reign all over the worlds, and they will love us for it."

Back at Easter's palace, they look in on Chris walking. He looks tired and thirsty. "Do you think he will even make it to the leprechaun's bridge?"

"He will be fine, my dear. Just give him some time and strength he will make it there." Easter spoke to Rabbit about it but hope until the end when all are aware of Chris. "Finally! He's almost there. I saw this part in my dream last week."

"Oh, Rabbit, keep it cool. The leprechaun will serve us well."

"Oh, but, Easter, he is still fragile from life."

"Maybe so but the leprechaun will be very gentle, I believe."

"He will. I just hope Chris's eyes don't scare his mind and emotions from his appearance my mother."

As Chris walked he started to see the bridge nearby. "Oh sweet Jesus! There it goes. The bridge is close. I just need to get across without that leprechaun attacking me." As he got closer to the bridge a little person was watching Chris. He was a green little man. With a green suit on and a feathered green hat.

He said, "I know he's after me gold. Just a few more steps and . . ." Chris took four more steps and then fell down a ditch. He didn't break anything though, but he sure was upset.

"What in God's name is this? I can't live a good life without hell coming down on me!"

"Cheer up for a little while. This will only take a second. I want to ask you something, and I don't want you to lie to me. Were ya going to try and steal me gold? Yes or no."

"Gold! I don't need any gold right now, Mr . . . ."

"Well, I told you don't lie to me. And now I will kill you and eat you for my dinner next week. How about that!"

"Oh, mister, that won't be necessary. See I have to get home to my wife soon. I don't really belong here . . ."

"Don't give me any bull! You try to steal me gold and got caught at it."

"Please, mister . . ."

"The name's Mr. Reldoph to you. And I have to tell you . . . you're a softy."

"If there's anything I can do to get out of this mess, let me know and I'll do it."

Mr. Reldoph looked around and said, "Listen in . . . If you can figure this riddle I'll let you go . . . I have been working on something. It's kind of difficult for me to finish. You know us leprechauns use all of our gold to make worlds. Tell me . . . what do you need to create a world?"

He stood there in the ditch. "What kind of question is that? Oh, where to begin . . ."

"All I need is two words."

As he thought he began putting two and two together. "I got it . . . nucleus bombs! When a nucleus bomb hits the core of our moon it sends gravity to that part for tree production for oxygen and H2O. Am I correct?" Mr. Reldoph looks at him for a second and then began to laugh.

"That's correct, young man, correct! I'll let you pass my bridge, kind man. That shows you're a God-fearing man, you do not steal." He throws a ladder down for Chris. He climbs up it. "Very good . . . What is your name, by the way?"

"Oh, it's Chris."

"You're the creator of that flying machine. The Clause, right? You just got here. Without dying, huh?"

"Yes, I'm him."

"Yes. We're all talking about you. You got a date with the devil himself, the king of Halloween, huh? Guy. Do you think you can beat 'em because I don't think so. He'll scare you so bad you will faint to death. He's a force to be reckoned with. What are ya going to do?"

"I don't know, but I need to get out of here."

"What do you mean? You just got here. Cheer up, lad. There's a lot to do in our world Holiday today and forever. Maybe you don't know that yet. You being a live one and all. You don't get our transition. Yours come from Earth. Well, this is our paradise, and you're welcome in my book of goodness. Now you need to find Captain Hopkins too. He should be across my bridge. Get him and get him good. He seems to never pay me my fare for my bridge here."

"I'll do my best even if I'm scared to death about it."

"Good! Cause you would rather die from Hopkins instead of by Guy of Halloween!"

"Who you telling? I already know I'm doomed if I do, doomed if I don't. All I need is my time machine to fly up and see Mother Easter. Oh I wonder how she looks. Like a little Bunny or a human Bunny? I have to see that even if that kills me."

"You're lucky Easter don't kill. Right?"

"Sure thing."

As Chris walks away Mr. Reldoph says, "Oh, and be careful the April Fool's Kids are out for the attack to gain Guy's heart. From now on do not trust anybody!"

"Sure thing. I'll see ya!" Chris yelled out. As he turned he felt he had no choice but to dread this day in the world Holiday. With the army soldiers of Memorial Day taking his time machine on sleighs, a human-size hog telling him about hell on Holiday, a leprechaun wanting to charge him for taking gold he didn't take, and Guy of Halloween trying to kill him, it pretty much has been a sleazy and, don't forget, horrific day. And still there is more to come.

All of these characters do have a significance—they all come from the holidays of his nation, America. All through the calendar. What are they? And why are they stringing him along a journey he doesn't want. But still, Chris is Chris, and he will succeed this story they made for him. And for all sake he must make it back to his wife.

He has no communication with her right now, and that's eating him up. He knows she's just in some corner in the house crying her eyes out. He has no idea what's going on without his time machine, the Clause. And as long as he doesn't have it he will be lost.

He has a few more tasks to complete and then he can go home. But if he doesn't succeed and gets killed, well, you know the rest. He will succeed still. But lose everything first . . .

"Mr. Reldoph was very nice to me. A little confusing but quite okay. Now I must find these soldiers of Memorial Day. Memorial Day heroes trying to rob me—go figure that out because I can't! I wonder if they messed around with my Clause any more. Well, I hope not. They're the most valuable equipment in my sleigh. It can do all things. And whether I have to fight a duel to the death with Guy or not, I'm surely going to try and kill him first. Like I said, my sleigh can do almost anything for me, and I know how to work that thing better than anyone, I tell you that much . . ."

He fell in another ditch made by the April Fool's Kids. "Did ya think you were going to be treated like how Mr. Reldoph treated you? There's another thing coming to ya, pal!" Ak, Po, and To began laughing at Chris; this time he hurt his arm and he needs help now. What is he going to do against these little ugly-looking children with their deep, scratchy, grown-people voices scaring the holiday out of Chris?

3

The Healing Spell!

"SO, MR. CHRIS . . . Yeah, we know your name already. How about you killing yourself for the sake of our pal Guy? You know 'em—of Halloween? Do you want to stay down their injured?"

"No! No! Please I'll do anything. Just get me out of here!"

"No! First you got to . . . make us a time machine, man! You can do that for us. Because the way they described your flying object, it's a beauty and we want in on it!"

As he was stuck in that ditch he wondered how he got himself into this problem. "Come on, man! Give me a chance. I'll do anything to get out of this hellhole! Anything!"

Then Ak said, "First you have to kiss my grits! Then you have to finally reach the top of the hillside! Then you got to know what you talking 'bout, Willis!"

"What in the hell are you talking about, children?"

"First of all we're not just children. We know what you're thinking. We are April Fool's Kids! Okay, buddy, so don't go talking stupid! And secondly it ain't your business what we're talking about. It's way past your time. I'm surprised you don't know about sitcoms with your time machine."

Then Po said, "Yeah! Your time machine is bogus if you haven't seen any of the future yet."

"I just started this job! My fourth time out of my world! Listen, please, if you can just get me out of here I'll show you how to make one just like my time machine! Please!"

"I don't know, mister, but the best thing is for you to just sit back, relax, take off your shoes, smoke on some cigarettes, and rot in our hole in the ditch, buddy!" To said.

As the April Fool's Kids were tormenting Chris, Bigga and Bugsy were coming from school down the road. They almost didn't see what was going on with the April Fool's Kids, but they did, and they went to some bushes behind them.

"Ak! Did you hear something?"

"Nah, Po, nothing but him squirming around down there."

Bigga then said, whispering to Bugsy behind the bushes, "I wonder whose in the hole, Bugsy."

"I don't know either, but it has to be someone in need. Come on. Let's show these three a lot of fear. Let's use . . . impersonations. I think a giant bear can be their retreat." He begins to shout out growls like a bear. Then they began moving the bushes as if it's coming toward them.

"I told you something was looking at us," Po said.

"Oh! It's a bear!" Ak said in fear. The three of them began to run fast away from Chris. Without any hesitation, stuck down in the ditch, Chris began yelling out, "Help! Anyone up there! Help! Help! Help!" As soon as the two bunnies came, he felt relieved.

"Hold your horses, Doc. It's about too early for all that yelling, don't you think?"

"Besides, we don't even know ya, man!" Bigga said after Bugsy. They looked down the hole and saw that it was Chris of the Clause!

"Hey, Bugsy, look."

"Well, look here! It's young Santa all Holiday is talking about." They looked a little excited. "Oh, Mother's going to love us for this one. Come on! Let's get him out of that hole!"

"Oh God! Thank you so much for helping, my little talking, human-looking Bunnies."

"Hey, watch that bulb. You know you break easy."

"Sorry," Chris said to Bigga. "But I've been through hell and back in just the day. Imagine the rest of it. I'll be dog food for the canines."

"Don't worry, we got your side. First we need to take you to Mother Easter. Then we . . ."

"No! No! Wait, we first have to find my time machine. That's the most important part of it all! If Mother Easter don't have that for me then I must go to who do you know."

Bugsy replied, "So you're telling me that you don't know where your time machine is at?"

"No. The Memorial soldiers have it. I don't know what is truly happening, but I want out of this now."

Bigga then said, "He needs some help fast, little bro."

"Yeah, that's true. We need to take him to see the general. Maybe he can get his time machine back."

"Then after that I have to fight a duel to death with Guy from Halloween. Boy, I don't want to die anytime anywhere!"

Bugsy said, "Don't you havc a full schedule for today, man. What's your name?"

"Chris Cringle."

"Bugsy, and this is my older bro, Bigga."

"Well, I need to get out of here first of, all right? So please help me." As Bigga looked at Bugsy, they jumped down there with him. Bugsy got on Bigga's back.

"Climb, Chris, come on, it's easy." He climbs out.

"Thanks, guys . . . Ouch! My arm."

"Be careful, okay. We have some healing potion for you once we get to the top. Okay, Chris?"

"Sure thing. Hey, how do you make a healing potion?" As he climbs out of the hole, Bugsy and Bigga both were already out of it. "What in the world! Well, anyway . . . you will help me find my machine then your mother and then home before the fight to the duel with Guy?"

"Sure thing. But I don't know about leaving. You didn't hear? Everyone here knows about you. You're the Santa Clause. They have a great plan for you. You're not going anywhere really."

"What!"

"Yeah! Santa, I want my toys to come to life as well, and some people don't have any toys to play with."

"Yeah, Bigga. And some don't deserve any, you know, Doc. So life just became sweeter with you. Hey, Doc. What's up with the red? Can't your suit turn into like blue or pink or something? Yeah, maybe a different color suit for each world, right? That'll be great right, Doc?"

"Wait a minute! You mean to tell me you all want to keep me here!" He gets faint and decides to run for dear life. But he didn't get too far.

The two bunnies caught up to him just before a trap was to spring on him from the Indians and cowboys of Thanksgiving. But they didn't see it yet. "Hey, Bigga, look . . ." Bugsy saw the trap to pull Chris up to the tree branches with rope.

Chris says, "What? What can possibly go wrong now?"

"Yeah, I see it. Let's go over here. It's safer."

"Let's go, Santa." They slowly walked toward the left and saw the rope tied to the other tree. "Let's work fast!" The two instantly untied the rope and attached it to the tree far north. Then they hopped back to Chris. "Now watch this . . . Five, four, three, two, one . . ." Then four ropes caught four Indians, and two cowboys came out with their guns out. Shooting in the sky! One of the cowboys spoke.

"What in the insane blaze is this varmints? Get my Indian soldiers down from there."

"We told you before, Little Sam, we ain't going to be listen to your tough-guy talk, you hear?"

"Well, if it ain't Bigga Bunny blind to my gun here!" The two started running, trying to get away from his bullets. Going up to Santa, he says, "We'll get you later, varmint." As soon as his partner and him turned around, Bugsy and Bigga was there. They shot off their guns but nothing happened. Bugsy and Bigga dropped them on the floor. They looked down at them amazed, and the two rabbits banged them on the head with mallets. They fell with bleeding knots faint on the floor.

"Why don't they get it the first time?"

"I don't know, Bugsy. But we have to get Santa to the general. Come on, Santa. We have to go!"

"I'm right behind you. Now tell me more about this 'Santa got to stay' situation?" A little worried, Chris walks off with them to see the general.

As Girl, the wife of Guy, same name as her daughter also. Of green skin. Was cooking soup for her and her family outside, for they are outside creatures even in the snow their caves are cold. But they survive at all times by the moons of Halloween power. The mouths of their teeth are sharp as ours. Guy barges in angry. He saw the Bunnies interfering with the plan. "These little snotty-nosed Bunnies are interfering with the plan, Girl. How am I going to kill him before the moon tonight? Or how am I going to keep him here? His inventions, Girl, are remarkable. If he goes back, all will be doomed for him to leave. All he been through he can at least let me kill him too. Girl, this is unbelievable. I want him to belong here."

"Well, Guy, you have to catch him at a specific time, am I correct? And you have to really kill him, I mean like *pow*! Give it to him good. He needs to know death brings great life. He will be newly born to here. If it was me I'll just kill him right now. But it has to be perfect. So he won't hate me when he's born here."

"Why now, Girl? Could you please tell why now?" he said, anxiously sarcastic.

"Because it'll be your new daughter's birthday then we can take over holiday forever!"

"Remember, you tried it, and now you're on parole. Remember that! There has to be a way I can kill him tonight and call this day . . . Christmas. I will succeed in this and he will return. He witnessed something, Girl, and what goes on in Holiday . . . stays in Holiday. Plus he's from another world. We must make things right or Easter will fall. I know this. I'm first here on Holiday."

Walking on the road with the two bunnies, Chris repeats the same words. "Stays in Vegas! That's true."

"What do you mean Vegas? Don't you mean Holiday?"

"Sure thing. I won't tell a soul. First of all I'm a professional psychiatrist. I'm trained to keep things a secret."

"But you're not here for the great psychiatrist holiday, you're here for the Santa Clause holiday—Christmas."

"What! That sounds wonderful . . ."

"But you still got to die though, sad thing about it."

"What! Wait a minute, this can't be . . ."

As they walk off, Easter looks on in her wishing fountain of fresh clear water spinning in a whirlwind constantly flushing down. "My two boys Rabbit what help they can do for him in the forest. I bet they can help him get his time machine back. Then he can come to see me. His entire gift is waiting. He does not have to stay by death in my hands. No. He will just have to hurry up before Guy gets to him. My Bunnies can do the job with him. Rabbit, look at your brethren Bunnies. They will help him."

"No! Mother, they can't. He has to do this on his own."

"He will hate you for this, Rabbit. Do not do this. Santa will be our ruler, Rabbit, and there is nothing you can do about it."

"I was only hoping for a fair trial. I know I'm not the brightest, but I'm still the most handsome."

"All I know is we will have to work for him after today is done. All will know the Santa Clause."

While walking, Chris was still in fear about this fight and kill game that Guy wants to duel with him. He also has to think about being kidnapped by this world Holiday! He looks up at the pink berry vine trees in the forest side tree area. "I'm hungry. There to eat. Are these berries any good?"

"Why don't you try them and see how they taste. That's a better way to die than to stay here . . . Yeah! With poisons," Bigga said to Chris.

"Yeah, that'll be a way out, Bigga. But I sure am hungry."

"They said that you'll be fat after you die with us."

"But Halloween does not have to kill ya for it. I'll bet Mother Easter and the New Year lights can help you."

"I hope not! I do not want to get killed by any of you. I'm going to get my machine and blast off out of here," he whispered,

"What did you say?" Bigga replied.

"Oh nothing, Bigga. But . . . I need help." He swallows a clog of spit in a little fear. But keeps walking with them. In the far part of the forest two people were looking at the three walking. They were Memorial Day soldiers.

"Looks like the Santa is having a pretty pissed-off day," one said. "Sure thing. Now let's make it more horrible. Send in the Cupids of love and hate on them."

As they keep walking in the forest they see a bridge. "Another bridge! I hope no troll or gremlin creeps out."

"Don't worry, Mr. Clause. We won't mess up your fine dress."

"Yeah, we got better things to do other than that!"

"Listen, I don't even know what you two are talking about. As a matter of fact I don't even care what you guys are talking about! Why don't you guys just back off, okay!"

"If you really want us to back off all you have to do is say so! We don't want the Santa here getting all mushy," Bugsy said.

Bigga replied, "Plus, if it wasn't for Mother Easter to ask of you to come here for the December holiday we wouldn't even care about ya!"

"Wait a minute! You mean to tell me that I'm here because of your mother! What in the hell!"

"Don't go speaking my dear mother's name in vain. I'll clobber you."

"Bigga, no! There is something messing with us, and I think I found them . . ."

In the tree branches were two little Cupids flying on top the branches laughing and throwing "hate-you" arrows at them. They did not notice Chris, Bugsy, and Bigga spotting them.

"Looking at 'em, Brother Tant. Got 'em all cockeyed in hate with these hate-you arrows."

"Yes, indeed, my brother, true hunters we are for the light of the Holiday world we live in."

"Where'd they go?"

"I don't know, Tant, but I'm hoping the bunnies ain't catch on to us . . ."

As they talk to each other ropes fly around them and pull them down from flying. They scream a little for help. But the bunnies win again. "This should've helped you two with your shooting lessons. But now you're just tied up hanging around. The first one that hits the ground hits the target bull's-eye!" Bugsy said to them, tied up, hanging in the tree.

"Come on, you nice-looking bunnies. Let us down. We find you a perfect sweetheart for Valentine's Day. What do you say?" one Kupid said.

"I don't think so. Besides, working for those machinenappers don't pay off right about now," Chris said.

"Surely we're doing it for you two and only you two if you let us down . . . let us down, you stupid bunnies! Now!" The three walk off across the bridge, leaving the Kupids there.

They laugh a little and say, "You two Kupids are the stupid ones . . . ha ha ha."

One of the Kupids replied, "Oh, you want to use our special word, huh. Get us down from here, stupids." As the three walk off, the trees began to move. It was the Memorial Day soldiers coming in on them. In fear, the three look up. Bugsy says, "Run for your lives! They got guns." The three began to run but was sideswiped by rope-pulling traps taking up by rope and tree branch.

Chris yelled in fear, "Now we are the ones up in the tree. Are we stupid like they said or something!" This time a bunch of soldiers came down on rope to the three from the trees above them. One came close to Chris and spoke.

"Welcome back, maggot! What a mission you just went through. Well, I'm Captain Hopkins. I was radioed in that you would like to talk to me. Well, do you?"

Chris replied, "I saw my machine with you. I want it back now! It's the only way I can go home to my wife. You know how it is. See I didn't die to get to this world, but you all did. I love and bow down to you all. Listen . . . I have some gifts I would like to give you. But they're back home. You all are soldiers, so I have some weapons I built for the armed forces. I'll give you the blueprints."

The captain then said, "Then we can blow some stuff up on our base. Well, maggot, I thought about it beforehand. You spoke of the presents beforehand also. I'll give you the machine back. It's a little broken up but you will be able to fix it, I'm sure of it. So what are these new weapons called maggot?"

"They're called The P—twenty-two-missile launcher. For all your men. You can blow up anything. And can you stop calling me maggot? I'm not one of your soldiers, Captain."

"Good! I love a good toy for mankind. Let's go! Let's go, you sissies! Let's give the man what he wants. He got a date with fate. Let's go!"

Chris then said looking happy, "What do you mean by that?"

"No matter what you do you still will have to duel with the murderer Guy of Halloween. This is now written. It's now, not never. What I'm saying is our world now wants you as theirs. It's too late for whatever you were thinking for your self-esteem. You will be a part of Holiday. It is made plain. So all your crying won't help you now, maggot. Here's your machine. Work on it fast before your dinner for Guy. And see Mother Easter before you leave, or your future will be lost, best believe. Bye!"

The captain then pulled Chris's sleigh down from the forest trees and retreated more north. Bugsy and Bigga came closer to see Cringles's great invention. The Clause.

Bigga said, "Hey, Chris, is this what you wanted? Well, it looks swell to me. Can I get in it?"

"Wow, I've never seen anything like it. I like the red," Bugsy said.

Chris replied to Bigga Bunny, "Yes, you can get in, Bigga. Now let me see what's wrong with it . . ." He began to look in the back of the sleigh, opened up the back engine door, took off his coat, and began to go inside of the back and fix the Clause.

Under the sleigh he went. A few minutes went by. Bigga and Bugsy fell asleep waiting for him to finish. While under the sleigh three people walked up to him in surprise. Hearing them, Chris quickly rolled from under it in fear but noticed they were the three presidents: Abe Lincoln, Ben Franklin, and George Washington. Chris then said, "Mr. Presidents, what are you doing here? You're supposed to be dead!"

George said, "We did die. What about you?"

"Well, no. Not yet at least. I don't think so . . . but your lives were on the earth."

Abe said, "You seem to not be dead though. You're still alive from Earth at that. How did that happen?"

"From my Clause here. It's a time machine. That's how I got here."

Ben said, "Well, from the mess you made it looks like your cleaning it up quite well."

Chris then replied, "But Guy . . . he wants me dead. How am I to stop that? Plus, the whole world here wants me dead. I don't know what to do!"

George said, "Well, I know what to tell you. Go to Easter. She will be able to help you. But you will die . . ."

"Why!"

"Because you are a holiday or else we would not have met. You will die though. And with Easter it will by a harmless death. So go see her and watch out for that Guy. He has a lot of tricks up his sleeve."

"Thank you, Mr. Presidents. I will forever be in your debt."

In Guy's house the four family members are talking. Guy, Girl, Goon, and the youngest one. The sister, Gan, had to celebrate for Gan's trial and tribulation with Goon. Guy says while they laugh, "Hey, Gan! You was really scared, huh?"

She replied, "No, I really wasn't scared, Father . . ."

"Oh yeah, then what about this . . ." His face then jumps out in her face but his formed cuts and bruises on it. She fell out in fear but got back up quickly.

"That wasn't funny, Father!" They laugh at her getting up from the floor.

Guy said, "My daughter is now going to be a certified Halloween. We will anoint you today. Calm down, you two. It is time. You do remember the spell, right, Gan?"

"Yeah, Father, now let's get it over with."

"Yeah, tonight I will kill two peeps with one weapon," Guy said. "Now join in the sacrifice. The house hole of horror! Time never stops for us only because we were one of them in the beginning of the holiday. And now we will bring back the life of Gan Halloween. Lie down on the tablet on top the tabernacle. Yes, thank you, Gan. Now! I will say a few words, and I will sacrifice, then I will give you a new body and bring you back to life again. Like in the past!"

Gan yelled, "Yes, Father!"

Guy then said, "And with Chris I will just kill and leave Easter to take care of it. Come, let's proceed."

Ben then said, "Well, give me one of those toys you're going to give to the soldiers. Yes, something like that."

"Okay, I make you a supersize ballroom made of the best cotton to sit in, glass chandeliers made of crystal. And all the instruments for a hellified band. And you can have as many balls as you want at your white house. How about it?"

Abe said, "Sure thing." As the presidents left, he began to smile and went back to work on the Clause while the two Bunnies slept still. As he was finished with his repairs on the Clause the Bunnies heard the noise of the engine and got up from their sleep.

Bugsy said, "Hey, Chris, this is nice. Can I get in it?"

"Sure thing, come on." The three got in the sleigh as all the lights turned on. It sparkled the evening with pleasure. Chris said, "These buttons are for the time line here. It's how I get to go to the right time each flight.

This button is how I find the black holes in the skies and in the nighttime's space."

"This looks wonderful. Uh, how do you make your toys? And are you ready to make living toys yet?" Bugsy said. And he also said, "'Cause I do want my flying jet to talk to me and be alive."

Chris replied, "Of course . . . What! Wait a minute, living toys! How am I going to do that?"

Bugsy said, "You know . . . with that stuff Easter has on her shelf. The livestock of holy water she picks up every time she goes north, where you will be living. You know the North Pole. Yeah."

"Oh really, that sounds wonderful."

Guy woke his daughter up from the dead just seconds after a glow of green went around her body. As it stopped, she got up a second later, looking the same but different.

Gan said, "Oh, Father. I feel much better. More fearless. I feel nothing can hurt me. Thank you so much, my family. This is a beautiful day."

"Boom!" The April Fool's Kids Ap, Peepee, and To came in to Guy's house.

Guy said, "Now, now, my kids, what's wrong? Did Chris get his machine back?"

Ap said, "Yeah, boss, he got it back. You should catch up to him. He's flying now."

"I should, right? Ap, Peepee, To! To my helicopter!"

"This water. It keeps you all alive then, huh?"

Bugsy then said, "Yes, it does and it will you. Now come on! We have to go to Easter so she can decide on how to kill you. And keep you away from Guy until this thing about you being alive from another world is over."

Bigga then said, "Could we fly in this?"

"Sure, come on. Just give me the directions to Easter's palace and we are ghost."

A few seconds after they flew off a few reindeers came out of hiding. Their antlers long and sharp. They look at Chris's sleigh fly away. They walked and sniffed around for a few seconds and then one by one they too began to fly up in the night sky!

In the Clause, Chris navigates it. The two Bunnies look on in excitement. Then from the right side of them in a helicopter with huge bazooka missile launchers. Plus a cannon gun, Guy, and the three April Fool's Kids. They shoot out tiny missiles at them. Chris sees that missiles just flew past him, and in fear he began to fly a little faster. Guy still on his tail he shoots two more missiles at him. Knowingly he tries to dodge the missiles. In the helicopter Guy says, "You think it's I can't hit your sleigh, huh?" He then presses a red button; a machine gun came out of the right side of the copter. He begins to shoot the sleigh. Chris then pressed a button, and the bubble went around the Clause to protect them. Bugsy said, "Ooh, the palace is close by. Let's go turn left. And keep those bullets and missiles off of the Clause, will ya?"

"You bet!"

Guy just flew right beside him and said, "Hey . . . How ya doing over there! I'm about to kill you. I just wanted to make sure you know that! And by the way . . . take this!" Guy falls in the back of Chris. He shoots a missile at the Clause. But just in the nick of time Chris dodged it. He then pressed the black hole seer. Two popped up. One blue and the other one pink. He went to enter the blue one, but Guy was there first and shot a missile in the blue hole. It swallowed it up, blew up, and sucked in too fast. Chris then dodged the blasts, turned right, and flew toward the pink hole. Guy then flew for the pink hole also. But just as the hole got smaller Chris shot into time speed mogiulater instantly shot in the hole.

In the pink hole Chris and the two Bunnies' faces were pulled back as it shot through it. As it slowed down they found themselves in the desert. Still in Holiday. Bugsy said, "Hey, Chris, this place is the desert of the Eid and Hanaka festivals. We were told about over here but never been here."

"What time is it?" Bigga said to Chris.

He replied, "It's only one minute past. Like normal time."

"That's sweet!" Bugsy said. As they fly across the desert they notice the desert is never ending.

Chris said, "Where will it end, Bigga, I don't know."

"Well, turn on the juice again. Like how we got here."

"I can't. Used up all of it running from Guy and those scary kids."

"It's okay, Chris. Everything is brand new to you and you're not even dead from this planet but is still with us but come from Earth where many Holiday people came from. And the way I see it you're doing quite fine. Great even."

"Yeah! That's right. I even saved a faint from seeing a groundhog human size like me. But it's okay. If Guy couldn't get me then he ain't never going to anyways . . ."

"Well hello, Chris Cringle, as I spoke to some voices from your world today." In the startle behind the three were about six trucks and four aircraft helicopters the same as Guys full of Africans and Arabs with Guy on the Clause's tail. They were from Kwanza and Eid festival holidays. Chris then said, looking at the red button blinking all this time, "They pushed me to this limit. I didn't want to do this to them."

Bugsy said, "What do ya mean, Chris? How do ya get us out of this one?"

"Watch this . . ." He pressed the red button, and the Clause changed into a superpowered sleigh. A huge mother ship in the sky with two machine guns on the sides, two missile launchers on the bottom, and two ray guns in the front hood. They looked panicky but Guy was anxious to kill him. "You want get away from Chris. No matter what."

"Come on, you two, first we shoot the cannons."

"How'd you do this boss?" Bugsy said.

"Doctor, not boss. This was just in case of any trouble. I have a weapon for every world. I see theirs and I'm ready for action. And I couldn't have done it without your help. You know, getting my sleigh back. My Clause."

"Well, you're welcome, Doc. Now let's kick some butt!" They go off to the right in a U-turn for two helicopters. Chris aced the target of the two and then started firing at them the two helicopters the same at Chris but the missiles bounced off of the sleigh. Chris's missiles hit the helicopter right into two trucks. It blew up. The Arab floated in the pirate shoot in the sky, and the Arabs jumped out of the trucks. Now it's one copter left but with the second, Guy's copter. And four more trucks.

Chris then flew up in the air; the two helicopters followed. Chris then said hi in the sky as the bunnies screamed, "Here we go. And." The Clause then dropped down into the sky. As it came close to surface next to the four trucks the Africans of in two trucks and the Arabs in the other two. They start shooting bullets at the Clause with machine guns. Chris then pressed the fire ray gun, stopping in midair to shoot. It hit the four trucks after the people jumped out of their trucks for safety. It blew up to smithereens.

4

Another Getaway

AS GUY AND the other copter chased after Chris, and the other two Bunnies in his Clause they seemed to have no fear toward Guy. But Guy will try to install fear in them.

"Now what do we do, Chris?" Bugsy said.

"I don't know, but I do know they can't beat my Clause." In the helicopter Guy looked at the Clause in awe of it.

"Ah, poor Chris. Thinks he got the upper hand. I'll leave him be. For now but we will meet again, Chris. Oh, we will. I'll see ya later. Ha ha ha ha." He laughs as he flies in retreat. Chris and the other two look on.

"Where is he going? Did we win or something?" Bigga said.

"Yeah, we did, Bigga. You two can come from under the steering pole." The two bunnies went under there for cover. "Now that he's gone for a while I can find a light hole that's Earth and fly up out of here."

Bugsy then said in a hurry, "Wait! You can't leave now. My Easter wants to meet ya. It's the best way to die from here, and since you're here you will stay here . . . as a saint from Earth and Holiday of course."

"What do you mean? I have to just stay here and die out of my mind so your world can make me a part of it. Could there be another way?"

"See, Chris. That's why you have to see Easter. She will help you in the best way."

From the radio of the Clause, Mrs. Cringle spoke. "Hello! Chris! Are you out there! Talk to me!" He pressed the radio communicator on and began to talk to his wife. "Honey! I'm right here. Were you worried! Oh, I had the most weird time on this world called Holiday!"

She cuts him off, saying, "But, Chris, the radio has only been out for a second." He sighs and feels relieved that she wasn't worried yet.

He then said, "Honey, pull me in right now."

The two Bunnies were frantic. "Hey, bulb, you can't kidnap us." Bigga said.

Bugsy too said, "Yeah, that's a crime. You can't be Santa for us with a crime."

"No, no, fellas, I'm just boosting my Clause, that's all," he replied.

"All done, Chris!" Sandy Cringle reported.

He said, "Sure thing, Sandy. Now, funny-looking Bunnies, you gots to go. It's time for me to go home."

In the helicopter of Guy's he seen inside of the Clause, Chris speaking. He says, "Not today you will be leaving. Not today. I don't even have to rush." He sits back and watches the screen in his copter.

Chris puts the Bunnies out of his Clause. They said, "Not good, bulb. We can direct you to Easter, our Easter . . ."

"No need to . . . I got the Clause with me."

"Wait! Wait!" the bunnies said as the Clause shot off into space.

"Now here we are."

"Do you see any holes yet?" Sandy said.

"Oh, one will come up. I'm pretty much sure about that. Wait until I tell you about what I went through this time."

"I bet it's good and bad."

"No, only bad. The only thing that is good is I'm coming home . . ."

"That's still good and bad, Chris . . ."

"Oh."

As he flew in dark space night he then saw a blue hole.

"Oh, Sandy, I got one. In just two minutes."

"Good!"

"I'll see you soon, honey, and have some steak for me. I'm starving." He then makes preparations to time portal into the earth's ozone through the blue hole's suction.

"Here we go . . ." As he entered the hole he jetted through it. And at the end of the hole where he wanted to get off at he ended up back at Holiday's pink ozone layer. Just getting dark like as if he never left. But he was at a different location. He was at a piece of land with different people, a city just like his. Many people walked around as he flew over in secret. A voice came from the sky into his ear, saying, "My friend, who are you?"

"I'm Chris Cringle, and why am I hearing voices?"

"Because I'm wise enough to talk to you like this, huh. I'm Martin. Who are you?"

"Why you asked the same question for? I'm Chris . . ."

"Well, Chris, you need to find Easter I hear in your mind. Easter is far away from here. Besides, where are you from? You're not from here. Who are you?"

"I'm from Earth."

"That's where I'm from. They called me Martin Luther King Jr. then."

"When?"

"Back in the 1960s."

"Well, I live in the 1940s, kind sir."

"You will not leave until you die. It is your destiny, not fate."

"I guess I won't be leaving until I die, huh," he said in fear."

Sandy then spoke off the radio. "Chris, what's going on? You're not back yet? Where are you?"

"I'm okay. I'll tell you all about it in just a second. Now, Mr. King. I can get to her in this if you would just direct me the way."

"You reneged plenty times. Are you sure now?"

"Yes! I can't get away from this death. Might as well see Easter to make it painless."

"With you, my friend, all will be happy by this."

"I understand."

"Now you go east. The stars will direct you. It's nighttime now. Have fun!"

"I'm about to die, and he tells me to have fun. I'm scared to death!" He flies away to Easter's palace.

Guy watches on, saying, "I will get you one way or another. You're going past the Good Friday elves, huh? I will meet him here at the stalk forest were the vorhees lay Friday the Thirteenth trolls will take down that Clause of his there and I will watch. Then I will torment him until he's dead. Ha ha ha ha ha."

"Now, Clause, it's getting dark. We need to get there fast. Give me the compass navigator." The Clause flips it out. Chris sees the palace and sends auto control to Easter. As he came above the stalk forest relaxed he was sitting back listening to the skies for any danger. All of a sudden huge fireballs came from the forest, trying to hit him. It was the trolls of Friday the Thirteenth. "Oh! Clause, get into camouflage mode" He pressed a button and the sleigh disappeared.

Down in the forest as they shot out ten fireballs none of them hitting the Clause they wonder what happened. One of the trolls realized it, and they went to turning on the ozone lights in the sky to break off the camouflage from its bright light. In paranoia he said, "Oh! They seen us. Put in the force field now!"

BOOM! BOOM! Two hit the Clause, but he stayed in the air from the force field. "Clause time portal." He pressed another button and the Clause jetted into the night.

Guy was mad that he got away again.

"He has nine lives or something." He stopped short under another forest. He had to land in it. With a little crash he was all right. Getting out of the sleigh he fell to the ground from all of this. He began to cry. "Why! Why me, God! No, no. I don't want this." Then from the trees and bushes were noises of little elf sounds he never heard before. Frantic, he went to go run . . .

One of the elves said in a rush, "No, no, Chris, we are good. We won't hurt you. We are here for you forever. We work for you. Your our idol, soon to be Santa of saints! You are the last of the holidays to enter. And the greatest one also. How can you get away from Guy like that is knighthood. Are you a knight?"

"No, I'm not. I'm just afraid of getting hurt."

"Good! Good!" Out of the forest came about fourteen elves. Looking at him like he's God, they bow to him.

"No, get up! That's not necessary. Please!"

One said, "What's wrong with the almighty first Clause, Santa?"

"It was hit above the stalk forest."

"That must have been the Friday the Thirteenth trolls their monstrous. Stay only in the forest though. Love to kill things that come around their forest. Now your with us and we are with you forever. We are the elves of Good Friday, and we will be making your toys for you in the future. We will do everything for you."

"Wait a minute . . ." They begin to hug him. "Hey, do I have to die to get all of this?"

One elf replied, "Oh sure, that is what makes you you, Chris. You can do it."

"But by Guy, I mean come on!"

"You don't have to die from Guy. But someone will off you take you right out. Go to Easter. She has a beautiful death for you. She's the boss of us until you came."

"Then how will I get there now! My Clause is broken again. It's going to take me forever to fix this one."

One of the elves said, "Manny, go get the tools to fix this machine. Soon-to-be Santa, you come with me. I will introduce you to Mother and Father. They will take you to Easter. All will go as planned."

"Okay. Let's go. I'm ready."

"We will be fine now."

"We will be fine now?" Chris said. "Yes. Ha ha ha ha. Come, let's go!"

They went to the east more over in the forest. Chris was amazed at what he saw. Thousands of elves with their own little huts making new inventions of toys and others. The elf that told Manny to go get tools stayed with Chris. His name is Gotty. Gotty said to Chris while walking into the village, "So, Chris, your machine will be ready in just a second. You're a human, right? That never died in this world, huh? Well, do you want to stay with us? Yes or no?"

"Well, of course I would want to stay here. But my wife is on Earth, and that's the only thing I love the most. Plus, to die here to live here sounds crazy!"

"But, Mr. Cringle, it will make you stronger. All of your dreams will come true . . ."

"Do I have a choice?"

"I don't think they will let you leave, but you don't have to die by Guy's hands. You can speak to Easter, and she can tell you everything you need to know."

"Why Easter? How can a mother bunny be my savior?"

"She's all of our saviors. She helps out a lot and of course she can help you with your Guy problem."

"Then let us go see her. If she can do that I'm good for everything from her."

"Good! Why do you trust me in this ordeal?"

"Look at your place . . . it's wonderful here. You have things I never thought of to invent."

Then he said out loud, "You all are good inventors!"

They replied, "Thank you, Santa!"

"Santa, huh."

"Yes, Santa Clause. The owner of all the Clauses, yes, you are!"

But at Guy's house he watches them talk from on his arm where he can vision on anything. "This Santa. He can handle anything right now. That's what he showed me out there. Why can't he handle an old-fashioned kill by yours truly. Guy! He thinks he's gonna feel it but it don't hurt at all. I've died countless times. And I've killed too. I will kill him and Easter won't be able to help him."

Girl called him, "Guy! Come. supper is ready!"

"Yes, Girl, I'm coming. He won't get away from me, Cringle, bet that!"

In Easter's palace, Rabbit and the head light year of New Year's talk. "Easter, he really needs help in order to get to the palace on time."

"That is correct, head light of New Year's. We truly need to help him."

Rabbit then said, "But, Easter, he's done perfect so far. Why can't he fly here on his own? It'll make him stronger."

"No! In reality I've been helping him along the way, and he will find our palace then we will do the ceremony and his wife will not miss him."

"Okay then. I'll be patient. I just felt Guy will defeat the purpose like the other times. I have something for Guy as well. So he won't have any hard feelings about this."

"Oh, do you?"

"Yes, Rabbit, I do."

Now at the village they are preparing the Clause for Chris. As Chris stood and watched, Manny came to him with Mother and Father of Holiday. "They came from the world before Easters. Their shine is perfect, right?" They floated in the air, moving in a long robe. "Welcome, my child. This is Holiday. A world for the best to be at. You would want to come and stay with us, yes?"

"Yes. More than anything in the world. But I don't want to die from a painful death. And Guy is my fear."

Mother said, "Guy is the first here. But he also has been tamed. You will be safe. He's the son of Holiday. We will die without him and his family here with us. You must not be that afraid of him. He is the good one before us all."

Chris then said, "Why does he want to kill me?"

Father then said, "You are special, and he does not want to give up that chance. To be here with no death is wonderful. You came here in the best of faith also. But Easter . . . she can help. You just have to make it in time. Without Guy killing you."

"So all I have to do is get to Easter on time without harm done to me."

"Yes."

Chris said, "Then that's what I'll do. Get there in time."

An elf came up to Chris and said, "Do you want to sleep in the house till the morning? It is getting late."

"Yes, I do. They will be finished, and in the morning I can leave off."

"Then it is settled. You will stay with us the Good Friday elves forever and ever and ever and ever," they whispered to each other, Chris curiously looking at their actions.

"Well, I better get some rest. It's going to be a long day tomorrow. No wife to lay right beside me though. But I'll manage. Didn't expect little people would help a tall guy like me. Well, take me their . . . oh . . . um . . ."

"It's Timmy, okay, Santa Clause?" the elf said. They took him to a human-size house a few yards down. Chris was amazed at it. "Like as if it just popped up right off the road."

"Go. You are all right now. You can sleep anywhere you want to. It all feels like cotton."

"Wow! This will be a comfortable night, I tell you that much." He went into the house.

In the morning he woke up eyes first in red silk pajamas sort of like his red space suit. He sat up and put his slippers on red also. "This is beautiful," he said as he walked out of the room. "Hey! Where's everyone at?" Peeping outside. As he comes out further looking around the house he just slept in were the Friday the Thirteenth trolls guarding the elves with weapons while Guy came out of the bushes with Manny tied up holding the little elf up in the air. "What is all of this!" He goes to run off, but two of the trolls grabbed him up, sticking their weapons to his head.

Then Guy said, "Eh, Chris, how you doing? I hope afraid! Ha ha ha ha ha! I'm Guy of Halloween in the Holiday. I came for you, Chris. It ain't for friendship either. You see, I came to kill you."

"But why me, Guy? Why does it have to be me? I ain't the most lucky guy—oh, I mean person—out here. You get no points for killing me."

"Oh, we will see how many points I receive. You are now the Santa Clause. Which means that you're the last of the great ones of Holiday. Easter is first. But one thing . . . See whoever is the last one is everyone's leader. So I will kill you and show all that I am still the oldest. This will have me as your leader regardless for you will then be afraid of me always. And I will enslave you."

"But, Guy, I only have one life."

"No, Chris . . . you as a man have all the lives you need to be born on my holiday. You see, Chris, Easter will not be able to school you now. And you will then belong to me!" As the trolls laugh out loud, Guy says, "Truky! Lay out the sacrifice table of death!" They cheer for the new ceremony to become. "Chris will have his day with us now!" Guy said out loud.

5

I Need to Get Away!

CHRIS LAY ON the table tied up from head to feet as Guy comes out of the bushes with his sacrifice attire on. A robe dark black with hoodie. Black boots and his knife to kill 'em with it was made especially for Chris. Chris's mouth is taped up so he can't yell. The elves are watching on while the Friday the Thirteenth trolls wreck the Clause. "My creator, Grimm! Show me the chance of a lifetime! Grant me the ability to keep this soul here with us. Grant me his life and death! In the immortal scriptures of the great Grimm I will take thee." He goes up with the knife. Chris's eyes open wide. As he comes down, Chris then jumps up out of the bed, for it was just a dream. He was still in his bed, hoping he was still alive.

He comes out of the room and the elves are in the living room sleeping with their hats still on and in their pajamas. "Well, I think it's time to get up. Since I'm the new champ around town here. Come on, little ones, it's morning time! Come on, get up."

"Yes, Santa Clause, it is time. Manny! Manny! He's about to leave. Come on, let's get ready!" a little elf said to wake up Manny.

"Okay, okay, I'm up, you."

But then Chris said, "Hey, guys, I just had an awful dream. It was about Guy! He had all of us. And he was about to kill me."

Then Manny said, "Like Mother said, Chris, . . . you will be safe. Now come, let's get ready. You and I must see Easter!" They already got dressed and was ready to leave in the newly built Clause, the time machine. "I hope this works."

"Yeah, I hope so too. Now how do you want to go? Instant or slow?"

"Hey, wait a minute. What do you mean you? I'm driving my Clause."

"But you don't know my new gadgets."

"I don't care about your gadgets. It's my time machine."

"Okay, fine with me. Go on ahead."

Chris went to turn on the machine, but it wouldn't turn on and power up. "What's wrong with it? It's not working."

"Well, if it's not working it's probably because I have to teach you my new gadgets."

"It's not yours, its mine. My time machine. Okay, then I'll let you drive. Don't make this a habit, okay?"

"Okay. Let's go, Clause. Up, up, let's fly."

As they flew off they waited in the sky for a hole to appear. One came. A pink one. But this one said, "Hello, Chris."

Startled, Chris said, "Did the hole just say hello to me? Now black holes are speaking . . . I never seen anything like this world on Earth or the two worlds I been on so far besides this one. Ain't nothing better than this." Coming out of the hole in the sky, they shot out next to Easter's palace. "It looks wonderful!"

The palace had four points on top of it. Large windows. And each building has a round base to it. Manny said, "We can land right there on the forest plain. Did you see how I did that?"

"Yes, I did, Manny. Now can we go down to see Easter? My stomach aches."

"Ah, calm down. You will get used to her. And everyone else too. Especially Guy." But in the sky above two copters came out of nowhere and shot off three missiles at the Clause. The second one hit it hard. The third one hit it also and blew up the Clause. It fell to the forest trees, damaged not to fly by itself.

Chris was hurt; so was Manny. But they both were conscious. "Manny, how come you couldn't dodge 'em?"

"Didn't see them coming." As they sat in the time machine the two copters floated above them. It was Guy in one copter and the April Fool's Kids in the other. Guy said, "Let's see if their alive from that! I killed him, and if he's alive I will catch him and kill him. Straight from Easter's palace."

"Come on, Manny. We got to sneak up to the palace to see her, or he'll kill us from the sky."

"Come, I know a shortcut."

In the palace, Easter, Rabbit, and the first light year hole watches in suspense as the two, Chris and Manny, sneak past Guy's copters into the secret pipeline on the far end of the forest. Close by to Chris and Manny. Guy sees them on radar. "This can't be true! He's still alive. How could this . . . I'm going in to her palace and she better welcome me in. Easter, Daddy's coming home." As Chris and Manny ran into the giant pipelines in the forest two trolls appeared in front of the pipelines and grabbed the two.

They tied the two up in rope and waited for Guy to approach them. They swarmed on the grass, looking frail. But in the palace Easter was watching on her trusty the first light Year. In its rainbow orients of burgundy, tan, camouflage, silver, and blueberry. Light shining so bright but harmless to the eyes. But as they watched, Rabbit suggested, "He's still not in the palace yet. We can't do anything about it, Easter . . ."

"Enough! We have much work to do, and it can't go to his hands before mine. Now, Rabbit, listen to your Easter . . . You're going to fight him again, and I mean it bring it to him kill 'em," Easter said with pride. "Don't let him take our prize."

"Yes, Easter. I'll . . . I'll do my best to kill this Guy of Halloween."

He then picked one foot up and ran straight toward Guy as he was getting off of the copter still going on. "Well, hello, my fear fellow. How ya been?"

"Fine, I hope you don't choke . . ." He stuck a lucky bone in his mouth and pulled his skull and spine out of his body. As Rabbit laughed, Guy stood up standing behind him and tried to grab him, but Rabbit dropped down, grabbed Guy's arms, fell behind him with his hands above him, tied his arms behind himself, and split through his legs, snapping his back in half blood spill out.

Guy says, "I'll get you sooner or later!" Rabbit cleaned up instantly. Chris was dumbfounded.

"How you do that, Bunny?" Chris said frantically, afraid of Rabbit because of his effort to kill Guy like that.

"There I go again looking out for my Easter. Well how are you, Chris? And welcome to Holiday. You have many more to come. I mean lives, that is. Come with . . ." Guy then appeared with a knife stuck to Rabbit's guts, but he bent back to not let the knife hit him. He then instantly went into his pocket to get a gun and tries to uppercut Guy with it. Guy blocks it and goes for a stab. But Rabbit shoots off a loud sound from the gun. Then Guy went for the stab and catches Rabbit. He falls to the floor with the knife in the side of him. He then says, acting in pain for the knife he's holding between his rib cage and arm, "Then what's going to happen, Guy? You're going to just kill him like that. That ain't right. See, I know your turnoff button, Guy. I'll turn it off on you."

"You won't be able to do that dead, Bunny. He's mine now just like I said in the beginning of all of this when I first start to fate him deadly. Now you're stuck with the remsy knife in you. Everyone knows you're dead now any sccond. Now back to you, Chris. Wc have some unfinished business to attend to."

He told the trolls that were holding the two, Chris and Manny, to grab them harder for Guy to kill them both. "Hold them! I have two to untangle now." As Guy walks up to the two to kill them with his remsy knife. "The knife was designed to keep their victims' soul inside of it. If it kills Chris Cringle he will be Guy's forever," Rabbit said as he got up from the forest floor.

"Rabbit! You're still alive!" Guy said frantically.

Rabbit replied, "Well, you see me now and you will see me forever."

They look at each other. They charge at each other in a blog of smoke fighting. As they fight all the creatures come out to see them in the smoke. Bigga and Bugsy came around. Po, Ak, and To came cheering Guy on. The huge Hedgehog came out of the forest next to Easter's palace. The elves and the trolls too. Even Mother and Father. The presidents And Martin Luther King Jr. also drove in their cars to see the fight for Chris. But when Easter came out and said, "Not here, you two. Stop now!" the two stopped looking at Easter while Rabbit let go of Guy's neck and too Guy on Rabbit's.

"Yes, Easter," they both said.

"But, Easter, I wanted to kill him. He's not worthy to be the leader here. He fainted off of my child's resurrection in front of my daughter. He's weak, Easter."

"And that's what we need here in Holiday, a leader that is humbled, pious, and good."

"And, Guy, . . . if you can't handle that what are—," Rabbit said, interrupted by Easter, saying, "Well, I can help it. I will kill him myself! But it'll be by my standards, not a gory kill."

"But does he deserve that, Easter?"

"Well, indeed he does even though his future has not become yet it will still be. And with our help he can be great along the rest of the leaders of the worlds." Then Chris yelled, "But, Easter, is there any way I do not have to die at all!"

They all began to look at each other. Easter walked up to Chris while the trolls let go of him. "Yes, Easter. Is there any way?"

Easter replied but was interrupted by Guy, "Why, yes, there is . . . for I have a lot of goons that can change into monsters. I have one for you." And Gills come. Girl sends Gills out. An extraterrestrial with tough skin still a little see through. He looks mad but says, "Yeah, I will defeat you."

"Me! I have to fight. No, I don't fight."

"You fight with your Clause, Santa. Let him go and the other one as well."

Then Girl said to Gills, "Kill 'em one time and he'll be ours, I sssay."

"Yes, Girl."

"All right. I'll do it. But on my terms. I will fight in the Clause, but if I win I will get the privilege to leave off out of here and come to visit you here with much presents."

And Guy said, "And if you lose you will die by my hands."

"If it's a tie he will die by me. And he will live in the North Pole a leader of us all."

"I just want to go home . . ."

Easter then said, "Very well then, tomorrow you two will duel."

"Okay then. I'll see ya in the morn," Guy said angry.

Chris then said, "Hey, what's going to be your change?"

"You will see. Tomorrow. And I kill ya bad."

"Chris, you enter my palace. Come." The bunnies and elves go inside with Chris and Easter with eighteen new year lights. The Kupids also left. Flying away with their bow and arrows in their hands. Easter said, "Are you hungry. The servants will assist you."

"Thank you, Easter. I been through a tough day today, huh?"

"No, not really. You're taking it too serious, Chris. A kill is a kill," Easter said, looking stern.

Chris replied, "I don't care. I know that no one wants to die!"

"You would be surprised," Rabbit said.

Chris said, "Yeah, why?"

"Because . . . to make you strong for the fight I want you to know you died about ten times here on the Holiday so far. And we want you to do it again."

In fear he looks faint but Rabbit says, "Oh come on, you just seen me die about three times. It ain't nothing, Santa Clause Keeper. Your gadget is wonderful."

"What you're saying to me is I'm already dead!"

"No. you just die a lot!" He laughs out loud and says, "Come, let's eat food and drink."

"No, thanks. I already lost my appetite."

"Nah, come on. You just wanted to seconds ago. Cheer up. Okay. You have another bout to go to. Gills is on your case. I hope Santa Clause can kill him slowly like you did his father in it, Chris."

"Yeah, I did do good in that fight, right? Yeah. I need to radio in to my wife Wendy quickly. Where is my Santa Clause."

"It's over there bringing it in for repair on the elves. I told you to keep his war things in their for safety put 'em back in now," Manny said, keeping close to Chris.

Chris notices it and says while they are walking, "Why are you so close up to me?"

"No reason, just got to tell you something." He pulls Chris down and says to him in a whisper, "The only reason they want you here is to have you a part of their world. Trust me. They have wonderful magic for you up at the North Pole."

He looks over to his right in the forest before entering the palace and saw reindeers with their long-antlered epoches. They saw him. One bowed its head to him and then they flew off into the evening.

"Wow!" Chris said, humbled from them. "I want to stay, Manny, but I don't want to die."

"That's absurd, Chris. You will go on forever. You just have to adjust to living here also."

"But can I bring my wife here?"

"Why, yes." Easter then said, "After this you can for this will be your whole families place to stay."

"I guess I'm cool with that as long as you protect me, Easter, until I get everything together."

"If you win or if it's a tie I can do everything for you. If you lose . . . well . . . I do not know."

"Don't worry, I won't. His flesh against my Santa Clause, out of this world," Chris said happily as they went in the palace.

But Chris did not really know what was in store for him. As Guy and his family, people, and followers left, Guy said to Gills, "Hey, child of mines . . . don't kill him. Leave that to me. But I want you to destroy the Clause so oh Santa there can never go home again." They disappeared in the woods.

In the morning all came around to see Gills versus the Santa Clause in the arena next to the village. The seats were packed as the two was about to fight. Chris already in the Clause. It was flying in the air. And Gills was standing in the middle of the arena. The referee then waved the green flag to fight! All of a sudden Gills began to change. He began to grow into a giant that can fly. He then picked up his giant shield and his giant mallet. He was two times bigger than the Clause.

Chris felt faint a lot but knew he had to win against this flying monster. Chris flew up in the air. Gills followed. Gills was faster in the air, so Chris shot off two heat-seeking missiles. They both hit Gills's shield. Gills then flew close enough to swing at the Clause, but Chris dodged it and dropped down to the arena. Gills follows after him. Chris then stops the Clause in midair, turns it around quickly, and shoots off two missiles at Gills. They too hit the shield.

He came down on the Clause hard, but again the Clause stopped in midair. Gills landed on ground and swatted at the Clause with his mallet. A force field came around the Clause. That sparked the mallet on it to push the arm of Gills off of the Clause. The Clause then hit Gills with two robot arms coming out of it. Gills fell to the floor. Easter's people cheered along with Santa's new people.

On the floor Gills threw a swing at the Clause on the floor that scratches it on the arena ground into a hidden pit. The refs had some of the strong people throw out a ray-zapping chain whip sword. Gills went to retrieve it. As he grabbed it Chris flew up out of the pit into the air. "Now it's time to win," Chris said.

Gills also said, "It's your doom now, Chris. You're not Santa to us yet." The Clause weaved the whip twice but got caught in the bottom steel sleigh beam through the force field. Chris was caught and got thrown. While in the air he shoots off two heat-seeking missiles at Gills.

They both hit his shield, and he fell on one knee. Chris came crashing down on the ground. "Oh my! The Clause is down. I can't get it back up and moving." Gills gets up after the smoke cleared and began to charge at him.

"Oh no!" Easter said.

"That's my boy . . . get him," Guy had said on the other side of the arena seats. "Come on! Come on, baby! Do it for Daddy . . . Do it for Santa?"

"Vrooom!" the Clause's engine said for Chris. It floated up and waited for Gills. Gills did not retreat and charged still at the Clause.

He swung with the whip, and Chris shot out ray-zapping arms and punched the shield, giving a shock wave to Gills while Gills swung still hit the Clause again. They both fell to the ground. He did not get up nor did the Clause turn on. The crowd cheered in great joy of the fight in Holiday.

Especially the Veterans Day and Memorial Day soldiers. They all screamed out, "Tie! Tie! Tie! Tie!"

Guy then said, "He would have to die anyway."

Easter said, "Now he will be good and comforted."

But in the Clause, Chris was crying, "I have do die now regardless!"

6

All Better Now

NOW IN THE North Pole all are set; the reindeers are flying around their ranch Santa gave to them. The elves have over three hundred town houses they volunteer in to invent everything for everywhere chosen to go by Easter and the other leaders that Santa found out about after Easter had killed him in his bed in the North Pole's Great Palace for him hereafter. And Santa in which they all called now was a healthy old man now with a white beard. His wife Wendy lived with him also.

Do you know that in one death and life Santa was on the Holiday. And was born remembering everything of before plus he can be or do anything he wants by his law. He still goes out on December 25 to give presents to his designated routes. Does everyone see him? No! But Santa is heard about through all years. Guy of Halloween now respects him. After what he showed him he's worthy to stay forever on the Holiday. Easter was blessed by all leaders of the Holiday. And the people. She helped Santa through a lot of things. He can even create living toys, you know, like pets, but they are toys. They only last for six months though.

Plus, he helped make new inventions for housing on certain parts of the worlds that need him. And that was good. Back on Earth they celebrated him coming back home that night with the Clause but told his wife and everyone what happened to him. To see him off to live on the Holiday made everyone happy to miss him. They get presents too in his original city. Santa is known for his help all over the worlds. Plus he has help with his chosen company. The Earth and Holiday were finally united.

Now we will fall into another Christmas story under *The Chronicles of Lord Rivers*, Part 2! Now we will get into "The Town Who Forgot about Christmas!" by Joseph Mickey Lluvera . . . and of course after will be "Toolip and Airlie!"

The Town Who Forgot about Christmas!

1

Christmas Eve Night!

IT WAS A glorious Christmas Eve, and the elves are preparing Santa's sack. The reindeers are already being strapped in Santa's sleigh, the Clause. Inside each town house are the elves still working on toys. And in the main palace, there is Chris Cringle putting on his suit to stay warm in the space going from world to world giving gifts to the people. As his wife Wendy helps him, Santa says, "So, Wendy, do you think I'm going to come home in an hour with the Clause or sooner?"

Wendy replied, "Well, if you don't have to go to fly the space waves laid back and come home soon maybe we can have a good Christmas for us. Don't ya think?"

"Yes, I do know how to think. And today I will go to a new town. Easter said they have been really good, and I will give them their toys. It's called Tinseltown And if they keep it up they can become united with Bricksbee just on the other side of their town. But this new town won't prolong my stay out there, honey."

"But still, Chris, it would be good if you made it back quickly and safely, okay?"

"Yes, Wendy, okay. Help me with my boots. I got too big with all the elves' food they cook." Now as the elves placed Chris's magical sack in the sleigh it looks full to the brim but featherweight. And everyone's toys and presents are in that sack. Chris gets into the sleigh to shoot off with the directions from the reindeers routing route to all the kids and people for Christmas.

He calls the reindeers' names to get them to fly. As they went up the reindeers had to fly as fast as the time machine in the sleigh goes to enter a hole in space to travel world to world. Passing the full moon it began to snow. Chris presses a button and a force field appeared around the whole Clause to protect him from the snow and cold. "Now let's see what's out here to go to first . . . ah, Earth! We have eighty towns to go to and 1.3 million houses to cheer up. Oh well, let's do this."

He went to fourteen worlds in just one shot. It took him many runs to complete his route. But he went back to the same time of night to give them their presents. "It was good out here. I'm finished and I'm coming home. Boy, is it a storm out here!" he said, flying in the dark stormy night. He looks at the temperature, and it's very low in the sleigh. But in the sky as he flew by on top of a reckless town called Temper Town! Bullets hit under the sleigh. He heard the shots go off. Then a few missile came by him and through him off the mark. He lost control of the Clause. Another missile came by and hit the Clause down to his doom.

As it hit trees in the forest the reindeers get loose of the Clause's sleigh and fly away but not far. The Clause then crashed and Santa fell to the ground. Hurt and faint. He got up a second then fell down faint again. That same night a stranger came in the forest all suited up for the winter snow. He was with a little girl, his daughter. She too was covered up. Almost passing by him the little girl said to her father while noticing Santa faint on the ground, "Father! Father! Look at that a man in a red suit!"

The two ran over to his aid. They checked his pulse. "He's still living. But he's hurt pretty bad. Come. Let's put him on the sleigh. We can bring him back to health," the father, Manny, said.

But his daughter, Minna, replied, "But, Father, what about the townspeople? They will not let us!"

"Rest assured, darling, they will have to listen. I will not say who this man is, but I've been waiting for him a long time now. And he's finally here. Santa Clause of the North Pole in holiday, he can make this whole town back to health. Trust me, Minna, it will be all right soon."

They pulled Santa and talked about who he is back to their town, where the people ain't so good. They fight and curse all the time, rob and steal from each other all the time, and they set each other up in lies snitching in each other's ear. Now the only thing is Manny has been hoping that help can come on the way. And tonight his prayers have been answered with Santa. "So you see, Minna, all will be saved now."

"Wow, Father, this will be the greatest thing ever if he can help us do good."

As they pulled the sleigh with Santa on it faint, they came up to their town. It was called Temper Town. They lived five houses down and went quickly in the house with Santa covered from the little bit of people outside in the night. They made a fire in the house to warm up Santa next to the chimney. Manny then got him comfortable and cleaned him off any scares on him. Work was done, and no one came to bother them the rest of the night.

In the early morning Santa jumped up out of the bed paranoid. Looked around in fright and went to go put his clothes on. Fully dressed he ran for the door, but Manny was there to stop him instantly. "Santa! No! Wait!"

"Santa! I'm no Santa! Who are you and how did you kidnap me!"

"Santa, I didn't kidnap you. You fell out of the sky when the people had their national holiday, Singul, where they shoot off their guns and missiles. I saw your sleigh. It was destroyed."

"Wait a minute now. I don't remember anything you're talking about. I don't even know my name! Who am I?"

"Well, you're Santa Clause of Christmas. A real live Santa. You don't remember anything?"

"Nothing! Oh, what am I to do!"

As the three sat down and drank some hot chocolate, they talked. "Some I'm this great Santa Clause, huh! From a long line of Santas. That sounds good, but I don't know what's it all about."

"In due time you will. In some cases a man with amnesia comes out of it in a few days, maybe months. But in your case as a Santa it'll be a piece of cake. Minna, get me some more hot chocolate, would you please?"

"Yes, Father."

"So in due time I will gain all my memory back."

"Yup."

"I hope that you are right because I really don't get it . . ."

A knock on the door startled Manny. He rushed. "Come! Come in the closet for right now . . ."

"What is all this, Manny?"

"I'll explain later!" Manny said, whispering. He goes to open the door while Minna looks on.

"Hey, Manny. I just wanted to know who's in your house because I heard noises . . ."

"Nothing, Brutel. I was speaking to myself again."

"No. I heard more than you and your daughter. You better not have no one else in here, won't just be getting higher rent you will be getting an eviction notice. Let me see inside." He pushed his way in. The landlord is living in the connected houses with them. Him and his six children.

It's the morning and no one is outside yet. But when they do there will be bullies all around the people. "Oh, that's good then no one's here but you and her. Do not come out until I tell ya, okay. The town's having a party and your people are not invited yet. You better work hard for me, Manny, you hear?"

"Yes, Mr. Prent. I will, sir." He leaves out the door and already two women in robes are carrying a gallon and a half full of water in their hands.

"Close your door, Manny!" he shouted. He did it humbled and went to get Santa out of the bedroom closet.

"Sorry, Santa. You have amnesia right now. No need to get you hurt while you know nothing about your powers and magic and all you fellow Santas out their soon they will come. Right?"

At the North Pole Wendy was paranoid of the outcome of her husband's crash. Some of the other Santas had already come. She's still on the radio looking for him. The Clause is destroyed by the missiles of Temper Town festival, Singul. There is no way to get in contact from keeping the time machine going. "Hello! Chris! Are you out there! Santa Anthony, he's not dead. The red light still is blinking." A red light on the radio blinks. "So will we find him faster?"

"That is a no the detector is shot! I don't know what to do."

"Just be patient once the other Clauses come back home we can search for him. Its only four o'clock in our time. They will be in in about thirty minutes."

"But thirty minutes is too long! We have to do something now. Before it's too late. He is the highest Santa Chris Cringle after the original of Broville Mr. Santa himself Santa May. So what to do like right now for my sweetheart?"

"I don't know. We don't want any more Santas getting hurt trying to find him without help from all the Santas. But I will order fifteen Santas of the ones who came in first to go out and find him. But that will be too little of a team. It can be a whole town that knows of him now we don't know."

"Okay, okay. I'll just wait. But for ten minutes only. Could you put the word out to all the wives so they can radio in on the Santas to the news?"

"Sure thing!"

"Good!"

At the house of Manny they were talking about the people here, and Chris listened. It gave him spirit to try and help the townspeople. From their landlords and owners. The poor has not a chance in Temper Town save Santa to help. "Yes, Santa, we are treated like dogs. Our payment is food and shelter and the check we receive is for the rent so there is no way we can get wealthy at all."

"Terrible! How can you stay here?"

"We basically have no choice. And if they find you without your abilities you will be in enslaved as well. Minna will help you get your abilities back. The secret with you Santas are children. You never fail to get a good child anything they ask for. So go on with her."

"Come on, Santa. Now sit down. I know this is the morning of December 26, but I think this should help. Let me sit on your lap and then . . . pick me up, Santa. Good. Well now I will ask you for toys to get me on Christmas . . ."

"What's Christmas?"

"Oh no . . . Well, Santa, Christmas is a holiday about you. You go to all the worlds with a time machine for the whole night of Christmas."

"When is this holiday?"

"On December 25. In the month of December children all over the world come to sit on your lap and ask you and all the Santas for toys for us and things for our family and especially parents."

"So I guess you're the first one for this year, huh. It's still December."

"I guess so. Now, Santa, I want a doll with cotton all in it. I also want a rubber ducky for my father. And for my best friend I would like a doll. But different from mine. Plus, I want a tea set. And for my father, I want all his dreams to come true about you, Santa."

"And you know what . . . I do too." They smiled and snuggled together, hoping for the best to come. As the party started the hunters just left out to hunt a hog for the town. The two bands were setting up. One on opposite sides of the town. The wealthy people came out of their houses one by one. Two by two and more. Their children also came out with them. Some were coming off of the school bus for them. But still in the houses or out in the basements were the poor ones suffering with no help.

But in the house of Manny, Santa and Minna go off to helping Santa with his power and magic. "So think, Santa, think. All you have to do is pick up the bucket with just a thought. Come on, you can do it . . ." Santa stands their staring at the bucket until a knock on the door startled the three in the house. The bucket then shot across the room the direction Santa looked. To his right at the door. It almost hit Manny. He shouted out, "Woah!"

"Manny! Open up now!" He opens the door quickly.

"Yes, Mr. Prent?"

"I was wondering . . . do you have anyone in here with you? We found something out in the woods where you had to go to last night. A machine like no other. It's broken and we have it. So if you have someone here tell me or forever hold your peace." Minna hid Santa real good, but Mr. Prent still could find him. As he looked inside the house they talked a little, "We are trying to tow it back here now! The hunters found it. We need the net and sleigh made outside now. And swear to you, so help me God if you have anything to do with this you will be homeless forever!" He looked at the wall to his right. Where Santa was hiding behind the wall in a secret door, Manny made to escape if things get really hard out.

Mr. Prent leaves out the door again. Santa comes from behind the secret door.

"Wow, that was scary."

"After all I found out now I have no choice but to get to my sleigh as soon as possible. I'm starting to remember now." He goes back in vision where he was just meeting with the very first Santa. He then said, "All is coming back to me." Chris then vision back when he lived on Holiday's North Pole with his wife and the elves.

"He just told me about the sleigh. They found it already."

"Then we just have to find it after them, okay? This is what we'll do . . ."

"But it's broken up pretty bad. You need another way."

"All I need to do is press my detector button to spring connection with my wife again. But I can't be seen. Okay?"

"Okay."

At the forest the hunters still are looking on at the time machine not touching anything on it the observe. Others are there too, waiting for Mr. Prent to come with Manny. But coming in the forest mist is Manny with the sleigh under the net to carry the Clause on.

"Go on, Manny. You and the dogs mush! Mush!"

"Over here!" the hunters shouted. They got there, put the giant sleigh on top of the net, and risen the net up, and with the dogs and the hunters they pulled the Clause back to Temper Town.

"Do not touch anything! We do not want it to go off or something."

"Why is it so red?" one of the rich men said.

One other said, "It's destroyed though. We won't need it."

Mr. Prent said, "But wait! There must be someone that brought it here. From the sky last night. Now he's here with us!"

"Ah, foolish talk. Why don't you see it's an out-of-space vessel that take pictures of us. Last night a missile hit it out of the night sky!" The agreed a little; some denied it. Some were confused. But Mr. Prent then said if so then why is there an empty sack here. Made for someone to grab?"

2

Santa Chris Caught?

PEOPLE THEN BEGAN to whisper while Manny got a little scared. Mr. Prent looked at Manny and said, "Oh, Mr. Ferl, I think I know who it is that can help our curiosity. Manny! Get over here. Now!"

"Yes, Mr. Prent. What is it? I didn't do anything! That's not mine! Please, Mr. Prent!"

"All I want to know is the third voice in the hut. Who is it?"

"No one . . . what do you mean, kind sir?"

"You know who I'm talking about! Now give up his name! Who is he!" As he shouted at Manny, a man in a robe hiding his face came close to the Clause. He then turned the detector button on for the other Santas to come help him here.

No one paid attention to him but a few. Then the man said, "It wasn't me, but this sleigh here is beautiful. Who made it? It holds my Clause up fine. Maybe when the other Santas arrive to help me I can ask to make you a Santa, Manny! Ho ho ho!" He laughed out loud in joy. All the people were startled and angry.

"Hold him!" They went to grab him; he disappeared and reappeared away from them to his right. He began to say some of their names out loud. They responded and stopped shocked; he would know their names. "Wait a minute . . . how do you know my name!"

"It's simple, Mr. Bright! I can do anything I please. And all the good get to see it.

And in the North Pole Santa Anthony is preparing the search for Chris Cringle. "Okay, my fellow Santas . . . we need to find our high Santa in the worlds of ours! Look all over his route and find him. You four will go to his last two worlds, and you three go to the two last worlds before that. And you, Santa Jacky, you check the other two worlds . . ." He spoke until one of the elves came with a note.

He began to read it. Then he said, "Okay! There has been a change of plans. Santa's detector just came on. We can find him a little easier. His

Clause is damaged. It's crying out for help! Now we will go to follow the detector. Okay, let's fly out!"

They all got up with their red suits on and marched out to the Clauses and reindeers to go out and rescue Chris. But meanwhile in Temper Town they finally caught Chris. "So, Santa, you thought it would be good to show off your magic, so little you have. Now you're caught. Who can help you now? Turn off that switch. They will not find our town without that detector on," Mr. Bright said devilishly. He knows about the stories of Santa and Chris.

He also said, "I know about your kind. The Santa Clauses of Christmas. I don't like your kind! You're the ones that hate on the rich for their snotty attitudes. You don't like bad! You give the bad coal for your Christmas shame on you! Put him in the whyme pinns and don't feed him nothing. Until court tomorrow. Now!" They grabbed up Santa. The amnesia took its toll on him; he could not help himself then after.

And in the sleigh of Santa Peter above fourteen worlds from the destination the red light and detector machine turned off. He radioed it in. "Santa Anthony . . . we can't detect his whereabouts anymore. Don't know where he's at. What to do?"

Back at the North Pole Santa Anthony put on the loud speaker. "Emergency! Emergency! Santa in need from harm. Pack up! We're flying out to save him!"

At that time the Santas jumped up out of their beds to get dressed to save Chris. Some older than him in the Santa business and eleven after his anointed ceremony. The elves was even up preparing the Santas to find him. They are going to comb all the worlds exsorsting themselves for a second trip of many days in one altering time. "Santa Anthony, we will have to do this now. There are about 194 worlds with ozone layers of color or some sort. Please, he's our most important Santa yet!"

Santa Rell said on the CD, "Radio to him in his sleigh out to find Santa Chris."

Santa Anthony replied, "Yes, but we must be careful. We will be altering time. Santa Chris has not recorded this time. So make sure you find him quick!"

"Sure thing, Santa! And out!" Santa Rell then flew off out of Holiday's pink ozone layer into the night space, meeting up with the others. About thirty-eight was out that morning trying to find Santa Chris.

But at Temper Town Santas in their prison hoping to gain more memory. He sits in patience. But at the outside of the prison is Minna placing carts on top of each other to look at Santa. She finally climbs up and grabs his attention. He whispers, "Minna! What are you doing here! You can get yourself and your father hurt . . ."

"Well, all of the townsmen want to kill you . . ."

"Oh, here we go with that again . . ."

"But all the poor here believe in you dearly. You must be saved to save all of us. Please, Santa, let us help you! All of the village people will help now tonight before they kill you in the morning."

In just a few seconds a rope goes around the bars of the window. She comes back to the window. "Stay down, Santa, okay?" She gets down from there again. Santa gets under the bed. And in a few seconds longer the jail walls were pulled off of the corners. Santa got up and ran out into the open village. As Minna with four other slaves got Santa out of harm while the Messrs. and Mesdames wonder how he got out of there.

"All of this has me to remember more . . . like my wife and things. Elves and a whole lot more Santas like me. I wish they can save us now," Santa said, running into the forest.

"Hurry! We will send you to the scariest man out here. They wouldn't dear to hurt. He lives way up in the mountains in a huge cabin by himself, but he knows that you do good, and Santa will come with presents he knows it they banded him out of the village. They never come to see him. We talked he will meet you. We have to go back so the heat won't hit us."

"But, Minna, my Clause!"

"Don't worry, you will see it again. Before the day hits you will be home."

He then goes off into the forest, hoping this man catches up to him to save him. By the time Santa ran toward the lake, he stops to catch his breath. An old man then came out of nowhere. "Hey! It is a Santa. And what is your name?" Santa Chris turns in paranoia to see who's behind him. It was an old man.

"I'm Mr. Zoll" he said, looking in surprise. "I think I'm a Santa but don't know that much. Have amnesia from the crash with my Clause . . ."

"Amnesia, huh. Well I can help you gain your memory back. Come with me. We have much work to do. We are going to my cabin. They will not suspect you with me. They think I'm the worst of their kind. If I didn't hear about your story about ten years ago I would've sold you out. But I know Santas are real, so come on before they think about bringing the hounds this way. Come. Hurry."

They doubled marched to his cabin on the other side of the lake. It was fast to get there. They entered it. It was a large cabin. Made for three people. But it was empty only for him. They sat down to talk. "So! Santa. I'm sort of like a psychic. I will tell you what Santa you are. The rest will be up to you. Now give me your hands." He then closed his eyes and began to think a little . . . "Oh my! You're Santa Chris! I see visions of you being the first Santa to meet the first Santa ever by Easter Bunny of Easter."

"So I'm some icon Santa or something?"

"Yes! You are the savior of Santas. You must have the amnesia wear off by the other Santas. Your powers will come back then. I'm telling you."

"I thought if the bumps on my head heal I would remember, but if the other Santas don't find me in time I'm toast!"

"It seems that way, but never fear. I will keep you safe here."

But at the village they just grabbed Minna and the others, they're interrogating them to find their trespasser. "Now we all know who did it . . . right, Minna!" Mr. Prent said to the four slaves with Minna. Others look on to see what they have to do to find Santa. "Mr. Prent, I do not know what you're talking about . . ."

"Well, your father's going to be tortured until you tell us where he's hiding!" Mr. frill said, bringing Manny to the front of the audience of people looking on. Manny was tied up on a crane bleeding out of his face.

"I don't know what's going on! Please let me go!" Manny cried.

"No! He's with Mr. Zoll," someone said. "I've seen when Santa was freed. I've seen where they went."

Mr. Ferl then said, "Let's go to him now! It's about time that we get rid of him also." The people stood still, looking a little afraid of Mr. Zoll. "Come on, I said we will have one big judgment day. No one will care about it, I promise."

One in the rich crowd then yelled, "We heard about this Santa person! He works wonders. And Mr. Zoll is a monster. For the both to like each other is crazy. We don't want any more parts of this."

Mr. Prent then said, "Whoever is with us, come on, let's go now."

One other of the rich then said, "Even though he disappeared like that don't mean we didn't catch him and put him in our jail. He's nothing. Come on!" They began to walk to the cabin in the woods where Mr. Zoll lived. But as soon as they began to walk, at the cabin as Mr. Zoll and Santa talked and ate, Santa stood strange for a sec, looking into space. "Oh, he's getting one of his premonitions or something. Or maybe his memory is coming back . . ."

"Woah! We have to leave this place now. I just found a leeway of getting some help. Come on! They're coming to the cabin we can slip by them and get to my Clause radio in my wife like I tried last time."

"Let's hope this works. Okay, I don't want them cleansing us from the town. Maybe you are immortal but not me!" They ran out into the woods. At the planet Holiday all of the Santas are patiently waiting for a response from Santa Chris but nothing. Santa Anthony says on the radio, "Santa Phillips, are you in!"

"Yes! I just finished checking out the detector beam and where it was coming from . . ."

"Oh, good."

"Yes, it was around about the Brettin universe."

"Oh, ho ho ho ho ho! He could've been on the lect, bring, and toopt worlds. I'll radio his wife to see his destinations along those worlds.

"Wendy! Come in, Wendy. Are you there?" A few seconds went by . . . she then spoke.

"Yes, Santa Anthony, I'm here."

"Well, we just found out he's around the Brettin universe. What was his destination there?"

"Hold on, let me check . . . oh, he went to two worlds—the toopt and lect. He must have been on lect. That was his last stop. He went to a town there called Tinseltown! But still something went wrong. Send some out to find him or something before it's too late!"

"We will once we get his true whereabouts, okay? Be patient. If he was in any danger, we would know. He'll get out of this situation. We'll help him out of this."

In the forest Santa and Mr. Zoll hide as the wicked villagers run through the forest with their torches screaming hateful curses. "Look, Mr. Zoll, we have to move," he said silently while Mr. Zoll recklessly eyeballs the mob.

"Them damn . . ."

"Mr. Zoll! You're supposed to be good, remember? You want to see Santa."

"Ah, yes. Yes, come, let's get out of here." They quickly moved away from them back to the village. As the people began to argue with the ones holding Minna and the others hostage, but they won't let them go.

Santa and Mr. Zoll look on from afar. Mainly closest to the Clause sleigh. No one sees the two dipping and dabbing toward the sleigh. The moment Santa got close enough to the abandoned sleigh, he turned on the radio. Then as he put back on the detector, he said, "I'm going to turn the light off so they wouldn't suspect it being on. That'll do the job. Come on, Mr. Zoll, we got some more unfinished business to do."

As the people was just about to disarm the ones holding Minna and her F\father and friends, Santa Chris revealed himself and took Minna and the others away from them. They were shocked to see that Santa was two steps ahead of them.

"Oh, you are amazed to see me, huh? Well, ho ho ho. I'm here right now in front of you. Take them away to the jail. Lock them up. It's a Santa arrest." They all cheered to his words of sarcasm. Minna then runs in Santa Chris's arms. And she says, "Oh, thank you so much, Santa, for saving us."

"Ah, you're thankful, Minna"

She looks into his eyes in happiness and says, "Oh, you're welcome anytime." "And your welcomed."

One of the people then said, "And what about our mob going to Mr. Zoll's cabin? they will be back!"

Then Santa said to himself, "God, I hope I gain my memory back once the other Santas get here like Mr. Zoll said to me."

"Yes, Santa Chris, that is the deal."

Santa said, "Santa Chris, huh. That's my name."

"That's what I gathered. Take it well I believe in it."

"Okay, Santa Chris it is."

Once he said "Santa Chris," red and green lights blinked on his sleigh. The people looked amazed.

"Wow, that's beautiful." They then went to join hands together around the sleigh.

One of the townsmen slaves said, "Let us pray to the Santa Clause and Santa Chris! Oh, great high ones, we worship you and thank you today for this fine gift . . ."

Back at the famous world Holiday, Santa Anthony is at his station in a chair asleep. But then the radio startles him and wakes him up. "Hello. Wendy." He looks up and sees that the detector light is beeping. "Oh my, we can find Santa Chris! Oh! Wendy! Wendy! I'm here."

Wendy speaks anxiously. "Santa Anthony! Oh, thank God I got in touch with you. The detector, it's beaming! Look . . ."

"I see it now. I was sleeping a little. I'm up! I'm gonna sound the alarm. They know what to do, okay? They'll find him now. Oh, I pray to the great holy Santa of the ho ho ho Santa Chris is all right."

"Thank you so much, Santa Anthony I'll listen on. Keep in touch." While Santa Anthony struggles to put on his suit, he presses the alert button.

"Calling all Santas, Operation Find Christmas! Please fly out. I repeat, fly out." Within fifteen minutes, about twenty-eight Santas were in the skies. it was morning. Almost everyone was up or getting up. The ones already outside of Bricksbee were going to work or home watching the kids play with their toys under the Christmas trees in their homes and apartments. But out in space all the twenty-eight Santas and their reindeers just flew into the dark sky. The light bubble around their Clause just flashed in the space.

In Temper Town though, in the forest where all of Santa Chris's reindeers where they ate. Until the sound of the Clause rang as all the reindeers bunch up together heard it. They began to float up in the air. The eight of them began to float up above the trees, their antlers proud back in the air. And then Rudolf appeared in front of them. But back out the town, they are listening to Santa Chris talk.

"And that's the story of the good ones. They never want to do evil once they get the hang of being good."

One of the slaves from Mr. Ferl said to Santa Chris, "So everyone eventually will do good."

"And good comes first, my young pualasett." She smiled at him; he blushed. All of a sudden all of the townspeople wanted to hear more, cheering for Santa. Santa then felt weary. He held his head for a while. Then began to glow. Putting his hands up he yelled, "Ho! Ho! Ho! I'm gaining my ability now. My fellow Santas are nearby.

3

Santa Knows Now!

"NOW WE ALL will help and treat this virus in your homes. We must be careful not to hurt them. They are still your families. We will help them believe . . ." As soon as he said that, the townsmen were in the cut watching one by one they came out of the forest threshold into the town next to where they had Santa telling stories at.

Mr. Prent said, "We must do something about this now! He cannot take our land like this. We own it. It is not right! We still give them everything. Even if it's not as much as we get. And do not get me wrong. They do everything for us."

"We see that, but it's a new day. Santa is here. We do good all the time. We want you to as well!" Minna said out loud. They began to cheer for her. "Then who out of us is with me and Mr. Ferl our mayor! Who!"

Mr. Ferl said, "I do not know about you but I like Santa! I heard a beautiful story. And as the mayor he is now officially in Temper Town. I never heard of a Santa before until all of this. What did you call it again? Umm where you said holiday. Yes, holiday. What is it again?"

"Oh, Mayor, it is a day where someone or something do something for you upon if your good or bad. See mine is Christmas. I bring gifts to the children first then greater gifts to the older. Like this: come here, Manny."

Manny came over to him; he pulls out a pill-like form. He then appeared a glass of water. They were amazed. "Here. Drink this. It will have you change complexion. You can change your features and figure. Plus you can change child or elderly like again. Go ahead, just eat it and then think about it. It'll happen." He took the pill, and in seconds he became a kid again. All the townspeople were amazed at Manny's change.

Even Manny fell to the ground smiling and laughing out loud. "I'm a child again!"

"No, but you're a kid now. That's what your kind is called through me and my Santas with me." And in the sky came the reindeers to Santa Chris in the middle of the people. "Oh look, my reindeers—Dasher, Dancer,

Prancer, Vixen, Comet, Cupid, Donner, and Blitzen. And, Rudolf, how are you this morning?"

Rudolf then spoke. "We were not able to come near you unless your memory came back by the other Santas."

"It is not a worry. I am with myself now. And the other Santas are coming to rescue us. The Clause was damaged now that you eight are here. We can meet the other Santas in time, okay?"

"Sure thing, Santa Chris."

They got strapped to the sleigh, and once that happened the Clause lit up in green, red, and yellow light. It then floated off the ground, ringing the bells on it. Santa said, "Minna, come here."

"Yes, Santa. Did I do a good job?"

"Wonderful! You are the best. And here . . . take this." He gave her a doll that speaks to her volunteering.

She said, "Thanks, Santa, I will remember this forever in eternity!"

He replied, "Of course! This is eternity for the living and soon for all things eternity will be, even for my toys. That, my friends, will truly be our paradise! Then he spoke out loud. "I will be here every December 25. I want you all to get along. Remember, we do not want the evil to approach us. By the time I'm back, all will be equal."

And in the sky the Santas were flying above Bricksbee Town all looked up to watch the Santas in a crowd shoot across their sky just from the night before on Christmas. Back at Temper Town Santa just flew off into the sky. "I will see you all next Christmas. Ho! Ho! Ho!" He then spotted the other Santas in the sky and met up with them. They let him lead the way back home.

In the largest palace of the snowy North Poles, "Many Lights City!" Dwawf the elf was running as fast as he can to Santa's office right in June. The little elf was shouting, "Santa! Santa! Your blueprints were correct a mondo."

"Yes, Dwawf. It's finally correct and ready."

"Yes, Santa, it is. The on and off modulator. Now we can turn anyone off to magic Holiday's North Pole and all good . . . if they want to be bad. No, we can just turn off anyone's control to our magic. They will want me to be leader after this. All will want it for their bad ones. Even Guy of Halloween would want this . . ."

Toolip and Airlie
The Quest for Paradise

By Joseph Mickey Lluvera

1

A Supreme Royal Icon

TWO SUPREME HUMANS who lived and died more than anyone. Only to help everyone live forever. They had many names each lifetime. They did a lot of good deeds in the face of evil and disrespect. In the year 2,700,280, they saved the duterod whole world from earthquakes, tornadoes, and tsunamis. They made a "rock the world to sleep" machine. It was made out of a crystal in the bulengy mountains. These crystals could produce living grenade. It calms down the shifts of the land from occurring.

This was their eight millionth life on the world. Older than everyone there. By lifetimes, of course. Him and his trusting child that went through everything with him. Sometimes he's better than him in lifetimes, but most of the time the first one wins. He got the child from the eternal life foundation. And they've been together ever since. Now out of all the lifetimes, books of the world, and how long a book stays, they found the last book the most interesting.

The last world was called "Freit" although there will be many worlds to come after the two made Freit the one. The world that will make them leaders. They started from the beginning of duterod, and now at its prime the two have taken over the whole world in leadership. They will be the first to do it in any world! Now in this time the parent is called, Toolip and the child, Airlie. For this time Toolip was born first.

They live in a huge palace with ten floors. It's as large as two blocks. And it has many rooms, about thirty. Toolip owns the whole world plus the whole palace. They will let him do his full life as leader. Plus, they will carefully find him again in his next life. And maybe the next one after that. As much as they can find him they will take him in as the leader.

He has four children and four wives. One from each of them. His third wife bore his first child. All children in the Freit must get adopted in or they will stay an orphan. He named his child "Airlie," but Airlie was not like the other children since he always felt to be the oldest out of any. He had a huge mind on the wonders of creation and experimented on it.

One day he was making projects as helping a hamster, a soft cuddly hamster how to talk in their language. Never before heard of so all began to admire him above the others; they foolishly started to have animosity. The people cheered once the hamster spoke four words to them. Then ten sentences. He was loved by many under Toolip.

How Toolip became leader was he made all things free, volunteering, and generous to all the human race by getting rid of capitalism. Their world the Freit bowing down to him all the crime went to an all-time low, for everyone had what they wanted with no cost. They were even happy to go to work every day. Free food, free transportation, free vacations, free work tools and materials, etc. Business never fell off, for all was free. Everyone, everything, everywhere volunteered their work. Money and getting paid was no more.

All because of Toolip. Him being one of the first out of the two there. And in this case by them trusting Toolip they are well aware of Toolip being the oldest of lifetimes on the Freit. Everyone knows his name like the Bible for the earth. His son, Airlie, is the first child from the third wife of Toolip. His first wife the third child. His second wife, the fourth child. And the fourth wife, the last child.

The other brothers didn't resent Airlie at first. They loved him the same of equality. The whole world loved and admired Toolip and Airlie. The two were the amazing attraction. As the whole family drove by in their spacecraft that float two to three stories high. Theirs is made out of glass, and it can fill up about sixteen to nineteen people. The people would scream out, "All hail Toolip! All hail Airlie." The brothers and wives would sit and wave with their parent/husband and brother.

It was now 3,412. Life was understood and at peace in the Freit. A world on a planet where all the worlds on the planet and other worlds only have humans on. This planet was the fourth planet to be put on its living system. The Goggle System; they stood and flew everywhere. They even flew like as if they were standing up. Time went by in a forty-two-hour clockwise. They had one ozone color in their sky. It would show pictures for each festival its day.

In the middle of the two triumphing above others they began to find flying rocks. Everyone was with this, but it had to be given to them by a bunch of chosen icons who found the life flying rocks in their forests around the equator of their world, Freit. The rock is the same kind of rock of the beaks of their lower racing creatures, birds. The rock pulls you up and about it destroys their weight and makes them lights as feathers. But they can go and come back but so far.

One day they tried to give the rock to Airlie. He had led the experiment. They placed it in his head, feet, and arms as everyone else but nothing happened to him. He couldn't fly at all although the others could. Toolip was in awe about it but treated him the same. Although his brothers laughed and said, "What's wrong with you, Airlie! You can't get up." Joking about it. Everyone said what's going on with Airlie. No one knew.

Another day they tried to place him in strength mode by pumping him with this syrup that has you as strong as apes. But that didn't work. The people began to wonder is he a normal child. All the great things they had for the royal icons they could not provide it for him. Peasants that bought it could use it to their best ability. Even though anything was free it's still a bye. As mostly every one that had the abilities Airlie didn't have any. He was intelligent in the highest manners, invented mostly all things their on freit but his body could not take in the medicines to keep him like the others in the world, powerful.

Airlie though was not worried about it at all. He was commonly still good. Since his parent Toolip was the leader of all the world Freit, Airlie was safe. His brothers were so upset he didn't receive his abilities since they were not as smart as him. Didn't hang with him or anything anymore. Airlie became a loner. Toolip; he was the one that took Airlie everywhere he went. And that made the other brother's furious. They didn't know what to do. do.

"Pharoah . . . I made some new inventions would you like to see?" "sure Airlie what are they?" Airlie & Toolip spoke. He showed his new thing's to him. "this ones a teleportal to anter city I want to place it their and in the blossim room. We and the other's can go their you know if they want to." Toolip replied to Airlie, "the more you get worried the more you make invention's & they work too! Well at least most of them. You never since to fail me my first." "I be good to them you know and just because I get sick from the medicine that keeps all of the freit powerful I have to be the out cast! I wish I did have powers I can help you parent and only you. Look at this other one.

It's a new type of air for us to breath in with lighter gravity much lighter it pushes us off the ground for work on another moon of ours. This time it'll be easier for man pharoeh. That's good huh." "yes Airlie it is. Tell me more about it." They talked and talked all the time. Toolip was never without help from Airlie.

One day Airlie was putting a atom together to hit it on some cement and lakes and his brother's were their finally; they never liked going to his science shows. "And when this atom explodes on the land their we will see a pull and push event of airlie in it. He calls this atom Airlie. It's surface it's water. This airlie will have us fly up and out of the world to torrist other world's. With the teleportal of electro's around the waste line as a belt on your garment then in this airlie you can jump and land safely in any other world you can reach. It's lowest formula will be from land to land.

"This is the new beginning of technology fit for the well-mannered. For not all families can go to this sight. The wrong must repent and prepare for their punishment, after we can help them back on their track. Here on the Freit. May freedom ring on this project for anything else is well-established to live elsewhere on the other worlds from the Freit," an announcer then said as he went along with the video on the large screen. The screen showed an atomic bomb of oxygen mixed with helium, magnesium, and hydrogen, with titanium. These mixers made anyone that can were the electro suit go from up and down safely and up to another world with the same product field. He's sure there are though to go up and down safely he doesn't have any problems.

"Wow!" they said about the explosion. Wild smoke filled the air on the ground and the sky. They immediately began cheering for Airlie! Even his brothers cheered. Toolip was amazed. As they were back at the palace, the three four-story buildings connected with one identical one aside a garden in between the first and second building. Many rooms many things to do and have. They we're relaxing eating while the servants stood fanning them; it was summer. "I loved your experiment, Airlie. It was exciting. So how long will it take to be able to put the suit on and fly away, Airlie?" Smogswell said.

"In about two months it'll be premature but harmless. But we keep practicing until we get better. The sanctity room will hold all the electro suits. There to keep your body parts intact. Instead of falling off of you going to some other world while you go the other way."

"Yes, Airlie, I think it's good."

"Oh, here comes Petel and Your Smogswell."

"Good, we can talk on how we are going to build it, okay . . ."

"Wait a minute, Smog . . ."

"Brothers, come in." They come in the room with Airlie and Smogswell. They greet each other with hugs.

"Look, the smart one in the family. He helps each time for Father. And like us, he does good," Petel said.

Smogswell replied, "Now we have to help build the machines at the site in two months, and it will be granted. Let us look at the green prints to this project. I want to help."

"Okay Smogswell I will. Petel hand me that profolio . . . thank you. Look." In this world freit they had a green ozone layer and their night energy was bright pink from out of their energy sources. Their light bulb's dish out bright pink also. And two other world's that are bright blue and purple in the sky they look up at.

"They look wonderful, huh? You are a god, Airlie. I love them. This will help so many people throughout the worlds we will venture on. As your brother, Airlie, this will be a great experience for all of us, you masterminding and us three building it all up from your word. What do you say?"

He looks up in the ceiling and then says, "It ain't fun without my brothers!" They laugh and hug each other. It was the first real hug he had from them in ages.

2

The Beautiful Project

WITH AIRLIE BEING the oldest brother, he felt the others were too young to understand him, but now they're working together with a beautiful project. But Handof, the other brother, was jealous but passive. He used the future pills to figure out that the only thing that this project will do is have a person fly up only land to land. But since he knew he said he only want to keep it to his self until the future comes. Handof was the youngest and felt more brainwashing from his brothers to do something like this. Their parent leader can be looked at childishly from such a project.

Four months went by. The project was just as Handof visioned. The brothers were insulted and began a new hate for Airlie. Toolip knew that it was only an experiment, but Airlie's brothers took it too seriously and ridiculed him from then on. Handof said that day, "See Petel, Smogswell, he failed once again. You see why I didn't fall for it. I told you both and still—"

Smogswell interrupted, "But, brother, we did not hurt you for it. This unlucky fool has hurt us again. What was it now, Airlie, because we don't want to hang with you . . ."

Petel then was about to say something, but Toolip came out of the dark with his staff in his hand and said, "That's enough, you three! It was his project in the first place. It's bad enough people are joking his name on this one you have too! You shouldn't."

"But, Parent, he is not like us. He has no blood for the medicine. He should leave this palace and go where those like him go!" Petel said, the one after Airlie.

Airlie then says, "Parent!"

Toolip then said, "No, Airlie, your brothers resent you, and I want to know why."

Airlie spoke. "Parent, we have a great connection, but the others don't. We cannot be too curious. They will still be with us. No reason is no reason at all they just do it."

The three other brothers said, "This is nothing, Parent!"

"Yeah, this is not good at all. We can do everything with these abilities. And he's going to die like the old ones. He's a demon!"

Toolip then said, "THAT"S ENOUGH!" He threw his power staff down and it began to spin. Toolip then said, "Whichever one it lands on will go to the other families palace and stay. Plus, this means they will betray me and hurt my authority." It stopped on Handof!

"What! This is ridiculous, Parent!"

"It is settled. My trusty staff told me this and you will go. Bellers! Fetch his bags and other sorts now! And if any other wants to go against me as if this is younger times they will leave also! Airlie, come with me. Now."

They both walked away from the three brothers. Their faces down but afraid. As they walked they talked. "Thank you for the trustworthy staff, Parent. I'm forever so grateful!"

"There is something about you out of my four sons, Airlie. Like as if you came straight from me. I will forever treat you well. Trust me. There will be hardship and exhaust, but we will prevail, Airlie. We will."

"Yes, Parent."

At the room of Smogswell and Petel, they were furious about what had happened earlier. Smogswell spoke. "This is crazy! They got rid of Handof! They should pay truly! Oh, I will forever hate Parent and Airlie. This will be heard of all over the world that Handof is not in the royal palace anymore! He's in some orphanage or something. To do this to your son is mad, Petel. It's not good. We should do things to get them back . . . and blame it on Airlie so he can be the next one out."

"That sounds like a good idea, Smogster. We just might be able to pull this off. To the olden times!"

They laughed and then began to plan against Airlie. "Remember, if he would put back the corberstablizer in the flying suits belt operator it would send any to any world! Here's what we do. Put it back in let him notice it then take it back out. It'll be all on him." They laugh together, hoping the plan would work.

At the flying plant in the desert Airlie was fixing his suit. He noticed the corberstablizer was built in. "I wonder where this came from?" He turned it on, went on to the surface, and he jumped up as fast as lightning bolts from the skies, and instantly he went up into space. Traveling the suit took him to two galaxies ahead. A world where anything can fly with or without wings. Going in it and landing somewhere hidden he went out to see if anyone looked like him. There was a few, so he came out the woodwork and showed himself.

He brought food never before he ate and went sightseeing in their parks and things. Airlie loved every minute of it. On his way back home he got there faster than he left to that world tentor from duterod. He felt happy as a horse with brown grass and burgundy hay. They can chew on it for days. And get full off of a few strands. Going to tell his parent Toolip the two twisted brothers came out. "Airlie, what is the rush! What is the rush, brother? Come, are you happy or what? What happened to you?"

"Well, I found some coberstablizers and hooked them up to the trusty belt here. Went to another world. Yeah!"

"Oh, good news, Airlie, good. But you shouldn't let Parent in on it. You should surprise him. It'll be best to invite him to the experiment. He'll love it."

"You know what . . . that sounds real good. I'll do it. But I need your help."

Smogswell replied, "Of course, brother, we won't let you down. But at the experiment to fly up to another world. His suit technician was ready for flight. By this time the coberstablizers were removed. As Airlie noticed it, he immediately stopped the show. The people were shocked Airlie faked it again. "Whoever did this is a menace we were to have had getting rid of the thugs and gangsters in our world. Terrorists were no more until now . . ." He made his two brothers look like hard criminals, but they were.

"Look, Parent, he's a menace! He does not belong here."

"Well, you two, it just so happens I found some ware coberstablizers in the newigy mountains just thought I'd like to give him his birthday present now than later, you know. So happy birthday, Airlie."

"Oh, thank you, Parent. It's wonderful. Now I can go back to tentor, where everything can fly. First you go to it for a few, Toolip?"

Toolip replied, "Sure thing, Airlie, let's get this job moving." Within two weeks after all of the people were flying world to world. Plus Airlie just when he was lost he made a wonderful invention. The flying magnet suit!

It was a breaking moment for Airlie and his parent. But not for the two boys; they were both kicked out and put in a more disciplined palace. For twenty years the four never saw each other until Toolip announced his step down on the throne and giving up his crowns. No one knew what was going to happen, but everyone was happy ordered by the supreme royal ones to never cry in greatness.

Airlie is fifty five and the others are younger. They came back home one by one all from a different palace. And still Airlie was the one to stay in the palace with Toolip. As Toolip lay in his bed healthy, Airlie stood at his side with his official attire as an officer. They talked. "Airlie . . . I will soon leave the throne. If your brothers do not help you, I will not be able to help. I will not be in office."

"I do not believe in to be in them so hard, Parent. We either become saved or washed away from our duties. No one can stop you from what you're doing, High Parent . . ."

As they were talking Handof came in unannounced and, with a foolish face, said, "Parent! Parent of the supreme seat, I pray that you gain health and lead us through. I don't know what Airlie will do without you . . ."

Toolip replied, "A lot, I presume, son. He is still the oldest . . ."

"But not the strongest!" Petel said.

Then Smogswell said, "And definitely not the one with the powerful abilities, huh, Airlie?"

Airlie replied, "I might not have it all, but soon I will. I already had the dream, and oh, it will come true."

Smogswell then said, "True nothing! You had not changed yet. That dream will never come true!"

"All of my visions come true. You three will never win. I will also have Parent's seat . . ."

The three looked at him as a fool, and hate was what they wanted to give him. To have ownership of the whole world, greed came out of it; they grew up wanting everything in the world. But Airlie was the only one that worked for it. The other three had everything but lost a lot of it by their hate, and they project it on their oldest brethren.

"Oh, tell me the dream, son . . . on my throne." He slapped his hands and Toolip floated up out of his bed. Then traveled in the house to the great room where the throne resides. He floated on top and sat down in it.

The others stayed back as Airlie did the same behind his parent. "Parent . . . first it was a nightmare turned beautiful dream. We were flying at the flying plant, you and I. For some reason you looked twenty years younger. Then all of a sudden the batteries went out in mine and I fell out of the sky. I look toward where you were. And I saw myself soaring up past you. It was unbelievable, Parent!"

"Very well then. Someday you will have to fly with me and my old counsel board. How is your team for the candidate seat doing?"

"We have a full household of workers on my campaign. New inventions and all, a new colorful ozone layer for our skies, and two new books out for realities focus."

"Good! Your dream . . . does it trouble you some?"

"No, it doesn't, Parent, but my three younger brothers do. I don't get it. I know what I am. I'm a natural parent and you are too. Time will tell. You're getting older but only getting younger. As long as we are together we will reign supreme."

"I believe you, my son. I do, but time is running out. The people where they lived at are behind the sons of mine . . ."

"But our people lived better and are behind us, Parent. That's all that counts . . ."

"But, Airlie, we are not the largest country. Actually, Smogswell's is." Airlie stood back to think a minute.

"I will pray."

"No need to pray. They must be good to the people . . ."

"But not to me. Not to me . . . unless my abilities kick in."

"I do not think that will happen anytime soon, son."

At the generosity ball mostly all the supervisors were there in this six-story high palace. Almost as big as Toolip's palace but made for parties. Airlie and the other three were taking camera shots by the robotic film paparazzi. The four walked in Airlie in the back of them for the three showed the people their musclebound bodies. Since Airlie had no abilities the people did not even look at him. He walked with his head down to think his brothers would win Parent's seat for the world. One bystander looking at Airlie said, "Cheer up, Supreme One Airlie! You're the brightest one of them all!" He walked feeling a little better. Then she said, "Oh, I pray his soul gets well enough for the treasures of freit to enter him . . . then he can take over properly if he can at that point. Life is what you make it." Saying it to her friend next to her. The four floated off the ground and flew into their floating thrones made by Toolip, magnetic pieces in the pavement's and in the floating thrones. They float anywhere you want to go. Just like a car. It floated them throughout the parade destinations with professional parade workers holding up their floats in their canopies similar to the thrones. Kafedy was throne everywhere in the streets. All enjoyed the four and the parent's parade each year. The three brothers only talked amongst themselves, not to Airlie.

This affected him dearly. Sweat, nausea, stomachaches came quick to him. His throne skid the pavement turning off. The magnets in both the pavement and the throne kept it from moving. The brothers just kept on laughing at him. Everyone went to Airlie's aid though; Handof felt ashamed but kept on going. Smogswell and Petel kept going too but with hate in them. "Still stealing the show, huh, Airlie? Well, forget you, Mr. Scientist!"

"The banquet is two weeks away. It's to show which one out of us will take Toolip's job. Yes, Airlie, I said his name. For the mothers of us look one of will be chosen out of two of us and two out of the four of us will be chosen."

"Yes, Parent said it. I heard him."

Smogswell said, "Did you think you will win, Airlie?"

He did not say anything. His head went down. He picked it back up, saying, "It's going to be soon . . . this election will be fit for the king of the world. I will win by a long shot. What you don't know is the future. I know the future. And you will have to work for me until you three are relieved by my leave. I am gaining the natural abilities you three do not have. It's coming slowly. I never told anyone. But one day I will show that I am more powerful than you three are."

Handof said, "Nonsense! It is a three-to-one chance. Either us three or you will win. That is all! I see that you have gone mad! All of your hidden powers are still not here with us. You're talking noodles. Leave us now, older brother!"

Toolip then shouted, "That's enough! This is still own to me. I am the first who owns the whole world. We will not debate in this palace! Now my Freit is a wonderful world not built for fighting. Now as I see it . . . the oldest is Airlie out of my family. Just because he's not with what you have and he's highly intelligent doesn't mean he's not strong."

"But, Parent, we are strong and he's normal . . . ," Smogswell said.

Toolip then said, "And still your brother is the oldest. You all have been taught to have equality in your ranks, yes. It is a fact that Airlie is older than what you three think. Life is a part of Airlie, and so Airlie is a part of life. A bunch of things that came first in the Freit's life came from Airlie. Look, he is one of the first pioneers that came forth in the Freit's bakery era. Where most of our high-tech inventions were created. Take a look . . . almost 4,024 years ago." In Toolip's right top forearm he used his fingers to turn on a time machine of moving images. They watch his arm while the commentator speaks.

Handof then said during it, "This is a good one, but if he was with the syrup in him then we could talk other than that . . . no I will not bear him!"

Airlie then said, "Brother, the syrup wore off, yes, but my powers will come from me, and it will be better than the syrup. And I will be able to give it to you by just a thought."

"Lie!" Petel said. "You will do no such thing. Watch. Your dream will be of nothing."

Toolip said, "You go your ways now the election will be in the eighth month out of fourteen. Our green and yellow sky will help both parties."

Handof said, "You better hope that your strength comes to you as fast as possible, for you will not win. Parent." The other three bowed their heads also to Toolip and said "Parent" with obeisance. They left; Airlie was to leave behind them, but Toolip called him. The three looked in blame to Airlie, but he did not budge to care. "Yes, Parent . . ." Toolip floated to the hugest living room in the palace.

"Follow me. I want to show you something in the huge living room where my main throne resides." Airlie walked there; the yellow rose bearers tossed yellow rose petals on the ground in front of him.

As Airlie reached the living room he saw a sight for paradise eyes: two thrones made out of gray sand floating in the back of the room, the blue lights on them. "Wonderful, Parent! I am not worthy!"

"Ah very much so. The three brothers still have a chance for one of them and their soon-to-be wives' thrones as you do also. But I have a feeling that you will win. I don't know, it's kind of tricky. I had a dream that you and I were flying together, but when we got to the end of the worlds, we kept going. There were more things to see we both made before. Bunches of worlds different than these world's, and that's it. I woke up. See, child, I believe. Always had."

"Oh, thank you, Parent. I just know I will get all I asked for now. Parent." He bowed and walked out of the huge living room. Toolip looked, smiling at him as he left before him. He then went to sit on one of the thrones.

At the Virginia convention the last debate was held; Smogswell stood there with Petel and Handoff while Airlie was on the other side of them. On the screen board backstage the votes were up. Smogswell had fifty-eight out of seventy-five, Petel had fifty-two, Handoff had seventy-two, and Airlie had an even seventy-two, tied with Handoff. The questioner asked a question to Handoff and Airlie. "This is the last question. What if the economy fell in weak energetic system. What would be the outcome and what would you do to bring the world back to high energy bill?"

Handoff spoke first, "Well, the first that would happen is a recession that will break a lot of barriers where our people will have to stop production. Their energy will then have become weak. I would bring an emergency two world closer act to bring our energy up. This will go on for two years. And it will form high energy to our energy plants. And our body will become strong again."

Then Airlie spoke. "Well, the first that would happen is emergency clinics will have to open for the weak or sick. We would then find cures for them by the deadline, of course. We would then place retired people in the workforce again to take the sick ones' place until they reach back to health. Production will then never have a stop."

The people cheered for his answer. Airlie made 75 percent in the polls and won the last debate. All of a sudden Airlie became dizzy and fainted on the floor. Smogswell and the two laughed. "I guess this is your time to go, huh, Airlie the nerd!"

One of the people said out loud, "Get a doctor, quick!" Airlie lay on the ground until the flying paramedics came to help.

3

He Is Sick for a Moment

IN HIS BED at Toolip's palace, Toolip stands over Airlie, hoping he'll come back to health. "Come on, Airlie. You are strong. Remember our life together. We are still the most powerful. I choose you only because we are always together each lifetime." As Toolip talked, Airlie began to say, "Parent, I don't know what this is, but somehow my intelligence is becoming much easier to comprehend. It's like I'm changing for the better even though I feel worse. My headache is painful, I can't talk that much right now."

"Okay, my child. I will let you rest."

Toolip left Airlie's room. He lays in a canopy of many designs. Smogswell and the other two talk. "Good for him he dies like the old times. What luck!"

Then Handoff said, "I'm a shoo-in now to win, for us of course." The two others looked at Handoff strangely.

Petel said, "A shoo-in, huh?"

Then Smogswell said, "Well, someone has to do it but why you so hidden like Handoff?"

"Nothing intended negative, brothers. It's just that I have the highest votes now, and you know that's good for me and you two too."

Smogswell said, "But the benefit . . . what of the benefit of us, Handoff . . ."

"I will see fit as the pharaoh of the world here on Freit we all will be equal except for Airlie! If he dies it will be nothing then." They laugh.

In the morning of Airlie's room he's not there. In the living room he's not there. In the other bedrooms where the other three used to sleep he's not there outside in the royal forts, gardens, and forests he was not there. At the flying area he was not there. At the energy plants, not there. But up in the sky around the palace none other than Airlie was flying without the flying suit on changing complexion in the sky as he flies around and around. "Woohoo!" he said noticing his great power in him. Going to land back at the palace Airlie looks four inches bigger, taller, and dominate. He's flying up in the sky with no flying suit on. All of his abilities come from natural resources. He's also bigger than his three brothers now.

In the palace his brothers are being catered to by two servants each. Feeding them grapes and bathing them in the bayo room. They talk. "Brothers! It is too late for Airlie. He's still sick. He's out of the race for our parent's position. It is all Handoff's now," Smogswell said.

Petel replied, "Yes, that is true, brother. We will all be safe with him on our side. For many years we were separated. Now we are back together. Nothing will stop us!" They laugh out loud!

Petel then said, "More grapes. Now let me touch you."

"Now we must pay our parent back in full for this position. Plus, he let Airlie get sick like that that. Ain't no turning back from that," Handoff said.

Smogswell then said, "Petel, I don't want to see you all over her. Give me some peace of mind, will you? Now if Airlie dies from his sickness tonight or tomorrow a sickness cannot interfere with the race."

Then out of thin air Airlie's voice came and said, "Disrespectful ones, there will be no more of the likes of you three. I am Airlie! The soon to be pharaoh of the Freit!"

Smogswell said, "How did you . . . show yourself, Airlie. I bet you are still the nerdy little one you have always been!" He then appeared from out of thin air in the flesh. The brothers were surprised at the newfound abilities that Airlie has. He was floating and then landed on the ground.

"Ahh, brother!" Handoff said as the three were in awe, trying to talk to Airlie. He finished. "Well, you were telling us the truth. Astonishing! I didn't think that could be possible. Life does evolve itself."

Then Airlie said in eight different voices in one rhythmic tone. "I am one with our parent that lived and took care of him for many lifetimes until all lived here by us first. And your doubt shaded you three into shadows." He then spoke one voice of a grown more serious voice. "Time only stops for more time, and that will never stop going on. But out of the creatures I am first and nothing from this world should try to stop that."

Petel said, "Then how will we win Handoff with this fine specimen before us. I change sides. I want Airlie to be on my side."

Smogswell said, "Me as well . . . I don't want my life shattered, but I want it natural and firm like Airlie. Never in this life or the next will I do this again. I want to be like Airlie."

Then Handoff said, "All I know is I'm out of the race. Airlie, you win. I must say I would love to be with your campaign. Please . . ."

Airlic then said, "Surely you do not get it, but I do, and I will teach you, my brethren. I will help."

As Toolip and his servants were floating through the walls to get to Airlie's room, he gets there to find out Airlie is not there. "He's well again. That is wonderful. Now he can venture into the campaign race for pharaoh of the world! A lifetime of everyone doing what you say to them because of your abilities. Even though my child does not have abilities don't mean he can't win the race. He's invented almost everything."

Airlie's voice spoke in the room and said, "Parent, I am here!" Airlie came in one big glob of smoke then into flesh. He then said, "How can your child be forever grateful? I received the best gifts ever! How can I forever repay you!" He cries in his father's face, not touching him. But bowing in his presence. Toolip, smiling, grabs a hold of Airlie to pick him up off the bow. "Parent, what am I?"

"Well, you are a natural only because of us being the best to show and prove. We showed we were the first to be here, and we proved it with our intellect. Now we must help just as you said earlier. A natural is given to us only because this stuff here in us two and a chosen few is not to get us stronger . . . it's for us to stay down. We are far too powerful. Now we keep the world going strong without flaws."

At the parade of the royal ones, on a giant cloud the screen showed Airlie and about forty-eight others behind them in their drop-top mother ships flying in the sky. The people cheered, throwing four different types of Kafedy out of their ships onto the crowds on the surface. In Toolip and Airlie's booth, Airlie looked up, hoping in his thoughts. He tend to look up . . . he saw only the green ozone layer. They called it the glow and the night. Airlie began to look surprised, and then he calmed down. A second went by.

Toolip asked him, "Airlie . . . are you all right?"

"Yes . . . I was thinking of placing another ozone layer in the sky. Or maybe two or three more to make the people happy. Each one gives sustenance, ability, power, and all we need out of the truth of happiness. Parent . . . I just thought if one was up there, why can't the others? Do we have the authority to do this? It has to be done already."

"What if it isn't, child? What would you do?" Airlie looked up and thought a minute. Toolip said, "As long as you are safe you can do all the good you want. Now let's find the base of the glow. Our green glow in the sky. We will help."

Airlie then said, "Yes, we will!" They laughed together in joy.

Handoff said, "What are you two talking about? I can't hear a thing." They laughed even harder. The screen shows the family laughing on the clouds.

In a desert off the middle west of the Freit was an underground skyscraper thirty stories under. They arrived in the Maybach ship to the site where they keep the ozone layer's main support system, the Tabernacle! As a tourist speaks to Toolip and Airlie. They all float looking at what makes the ozone layers and how it affects them. "The Tabernacle is a very delicate specimen. It holds all the planets and their worlds with everything in it. Come . . . this is the Tabernacle room here." The six of them enter the room. It has a see-through chest with dark liquid in it. They called it plymoth.

On the shelves are what they call Teepee's Jars of the same dark liquids in them. About twelve of them. And floating in the room are three different types of planetariums: one made out of water and clay, the other made out of of metal and fire harmless to touch, and the third one is made out of water and colorful lights rainbows of different colors within it. The water stays magnetically around the colorful light. The tour guide speaks to them. "See all of this is the experiment to all of our worlds we see."

Airlie spoke, "And what do we have to do to get the rainbow around the Freit?"

The tour guide replied, "Well, High Pharaoh, all it takes is one person to do so. This person has not been found yet. He has to be a natural, one not like the others with the infinite syrup in them. He has to be powerful and experienced. Airlie, if you and the parent are the first ones on the planet it could work as well. That'll mean the planet is own to you regardless . . ."

Airlie then said, "And what if we are."

"Well . . . let's see. We've been waiting for the first ones to come into our light.

We've been researching and experimenting only for these ones to be to give them ownership of the planet. Not only the world now we have ran some tests on people before that reached levels that you two had reached." He places Toolip on the see-through chest; it began to light up. "As a matter of fact this universe chest can decide it for us. You first, Toolip. It will determine how old you really are, and if you're one of the oldest you will be." The chest lit up in five colors. Bright as ever. The tour guide said, "Wonderful, it reached 94 percent . . . you are the one. No one has ever reached this percent before. Outstanding Parent of all Freit, it is great you can be it for us. You can be our . . ."

Toolip spokc. "Now, now, my Dr. Bland. I came here for my son to help." The tour guide, Dr. Bland, looked at him for a second and then laughed in gratitude. "Sure, Pharaoh. Come, come lie down on it. See if you're the one." He lays down on the universal chest. It lit up bright as ever just like it did with Toolip. "Oh my, Parent! He's hit 100 percent! Out of this world! Parent, oh my! Your first child is actually the first one ever to be on our planet. And possibly all the other ones too." Toolip with their team look at Airlie in worship. They bow on one knee to Airlie, all there in the room.

Toolip then said, "What happens next? Does my child learn how to operate the Tabernacle?"

"Your child is the owner of it. He already knows what to do. This was his long before it was an experiment for us to learn from. He will have to move in here the worlds will need him close to them. They recognize him now. And in a few years he will have it all packed down for the paradise of the Freit production. Yes, we finally can give our worlds paradise. A place to stay means no more death and passing away, only life and treasures to keep life going. Wonderful!"

Airlie looked surprised that Dr. Bland said he was older than his parent in the lifetimes before. "Dr. Bland . . . I have no remembrance of this . . . why?" Airlie said.

He replied, "Because of the powers keeping you down. But by your inventions and everything, your living proof is all you need." Airlie and Toolip stood there in greatness. After a while Airlie moved in the Tabernacle Palace and he felt the power in it each day become greater and greater.

Other people lived there too. They put Airlie in the pent house with plymoth. It had a see threw ceiling to see the sky. Everyone knew each other. They welcomed him with open arms. He began to be instructed on how to work the bed of stone plymoth plus the teepees filled with each existence in it. And also the tablets of see-through glass as hard as stone to see the existences in. In about two months he had it all mapped out.

"Now I have it all working for me, Dr. Bland. How do I get it out of there into our ozone layer? Our green color looks awfully lonely. We need to do this as soon as possible."

"But, Airlie, we have not the time to do it now. You scheduled it about two hundred years from now."

"Then what is the thing I have to do to make it come here early, Doc?"

"I don't know, Great Pharaoh . . ." Airlie looks into the green glow, hoping for an answer.

In just a few seconds he said out loud, "I have it. I got this far. I can go the distance." Airlie then began placing his self on plymoth, trying to connect as one with plymoth. The songs out of is of a live orchestra. Literally the songs show that plymoth is alive.

"I hope this will do the trick," Dr. Bland said.

Airlie lay down on plymoth. "I hope so too. I figured if I made the time for paradise on the Freit then I can alter it up to now. It listened to me then. It should listen to me now. Besides, It won't hurt me or anything . . . It loves me. Knew me for its creator right. The maker of paradise! I'll be fine."

Airlie said the magical words on plymoth but nothing happened. He tried again, but it didn't light up or sing at all. "Dr. Bland, what happened?"

"Maybe you need another . . . another force behind you. Someone powerful as you are even though you're in a class by yourself."

"Ooh, I have just the person for the job.

"Parent of all Freit! I need your service. In order to change our ozone with more colors. I know with your assistance it will work out beautifully. All you need to know is a few spells."

"Anything for you, Airlie." Now back at the Tabernacle they are preparing plymoth. They mixed the dark purple night like the night in their dark sky from the fourth teepee. They filled the Tabernacle where plymoth lay in with the teepee placed the tablet on top and Airlie went to lie down on it.

"Okay, Pharaoh, are you okay?"

"Yes, Parent."

"Are you ready?"

"Wait . . . I want to see if plymoth's all right." Plymoth sung to Airlie. "It's ready." The two began to sing a spell.

In the times of work to change the world
the colorful sky each planet's a pearl with treasures all in it as far as we see
the best out of plymoth for all to be
our work is to change the color to five colors
we ask you oh plymoth to change the simple world of many brothers
mind to mind
life to life
our world is not of hype
but it is made from all the light
now be in love to a new example to the story to make a better sampled story
Abra kadabra!

Then Airlie changed into stone on top the glass. Toolip's eyes began to praise as the sky blinked on five colorful ozones of green glow, blue day, pink berry, yellow shine, and white mist out of the large window he looked out of.

"What beauty it is. It's getting me extra powerful. I can't believe this." Toolip began to get stronger. A rainbow flew across his head in a halo. He controlled his sizes from grown to child. He changed his complexion to any type of complexion, even green shabien (extraterrestrial) But Airlie though; he was still stone. Toolip looked in awe. He tried everything except one thing to say the antidote spell to release him out of the stone. "Now the work is done so let him alive / a healthy child of mine" were the last words of the spell.

Plymoth song and lit up colorfully. In front of Toolip. Airlie then became flesh again. "Parent! What happened?" As Airlie said that a halo came around his head too. He changed back to flesh of more than a million years. Healthy and wonderful. "Parent! Look at you. Wait a minute I'm receiving great reflections back . . ." Holding his head's temple, his parent looks at him. "Parent, look outside! Look! From my thoughts I'm dreaming right now by my own control is coming true!" Outside in the sky were rainbow colors of the ozone layer!

Red, pink, blue, orange, and green. "Look at it all. It's becoming our place of stay . . . our paradise, Parent!"

"This is wonderful, child. That's first! It will forever be a great world with you."

"Well, Father, within two months I mapped out that reproduction of the world Freit is being generous now. *We* will have this paradise for a million years here."

"And all the children of ours will rejoice, Airlie."

4

They Fly Away Happily Ever After

FOR 2,409 YEARS they lived on the Freit's paradise until Airlie and Toolip became stronger than ever. The people too, they began to fly to other worlds wealthy and healthy they were. The tree grew two types of fruit, even three types. Flowers grew on trees too. Their rivers flooded juices from the roots of the orchards; the clouds and the colorful sky made movies for the people to watch. Every day was a holiday. They did different things each day to celebrate.

They knew every language known to them plus new ones never heard of. Their women on the Freit were gorgeous and happy more than ever before. No more diseases for the people, creatures, creations, names, and things on the Freit anymore. All was saved by Toolip and Airlie. They loved every minute of it.

One day Airlie flew to Toolip's palace to see him and give him good news. Toolip was sitting on his throne studying the ability to adapt to freezing weather and to not burn in fire. Airlie greeted him. "Parent, how are you?"

"I'm just studying some things to strengthen the body greater. How to not burn in fire or to adapt in the frost."

"Well, I have a surprise for you. It is out of this world."

"How far out?"

"Way out. Do you want to see it?"

"Well, Airlie, it's been a thousand years we stayed here. I think it is time."

"Good, I do as well. Come, let's fly. I think Smogswell will be the great leader of our Freit now since we are leaving."

"And they are informed?"

"Yes, they all know. And I think it's best to leave now." They flew out of the palace, going through the ceilings, and kept flying in the sky. Going through the five ozone layers side by side the enter the nights space. "What world are we going to, Airlie?"

"It's not a world we are going to, Parent . . . It's another paradise that we are going to. Come, let's fly!" As they reach the top of the nights space they begin to fly horizontal until they would find an entrance in the cave of nights space to the specific galaxy outside of their own.

"There it is. Come, we are to go in that one. I been here before, and I was strong enough to fix it up for you."

"But, Airlie . . . I can't fly any further. I'm getting tired already."

"Then here . . . take more energy from me. Grab my hand." He grabbed on to Airlie's hand. They both began to glow their rainbow colors of their ozone layer while entering through the tunnel of the nights space. "I feel much better, Airlie. How did you do that?"

"Since I been on the Freit my powers have become much stronger. I ventured in a lot of miracles . . . that I want for you to have. So I went exploring as far as I can go. And I found one for you. This galaxy will give you all you need to your beliefs to come true."

As they flew in the dark night with a beam light around them of bright red, a light appeared at the far end of their tunnel. "You see the light, Parent?"

"Yes!"

"That is where we are going."

As they reached the galaxy for Toolip four colors blossomed out in front of the two: yellow, brown, purple, and lavender. They were bright as ever. "Airlie! It looks great! There are colors in their night space how did that become! They have completed their quest and so have you." As they got closer and closer they heard the words louder and louder saying, "All worship Toolip the king of the galaxy!" He heard it and began to get surprised by it.

"Are they saying my name, Airlie? That's wonderful! Why are they doing that?"

Airlie replied to him, "Well, my parent . . . you had done a wonderful job on the Freit and many other worlds on that planet. Now those who seen you there the most where they are at is this galaxy. They know exactly who you are. They watched you, me, and anyone else that wanted to be like you all over the other galaxies. And they say I made it come true for each one on their planet like I did you. But you won, Toolip. Now this is yours forever."

As they went to the largest planet out their masses of people began flying up to the two. They had a huge throne for Toolip. Their planets looked like squares. They though were Angelites with or without wings flying up to them. Looking very different then Airlie and Toolip. They had one eye across their head with one pupil that had wavy lines on the sides, one on each side. Fur and feathers all over them, large pointy ears, and a pointy hairline growing atop their head.

One said as at least two billion came up in their space to great the two. Eight had the throne with them. "This is for you, Toolip. From our master, Airlie." As Toolip turned around to look at Airlie, Airlie already changed into one of the Angelites. It almost put fear in Toolip's face. "Airlie!"

"Yes, my parent, I look like one of them. And you will too." Airlie grabbed Toolip's hand and Toolip's halo changed colors from the colors of the Freit into the four colors of this new galaxy: yellow, brown, purple, and lavender. He also then changed into an Angelite. Greater than the others.

"Toolip . . . you come with us."

"But, Airlie, you not to stay with us?"

"I'm afraid not. I will go to the next galaxy and help them out as well. As you are my child I have other children out there too. I must find them like I found to you. You will be victorious here, do not worry. I will check up on you from its times."

"Then it is good. I will miss you a lot, and I will always remember you, my child, who is my older." They talked for a little and then Toolip left with the Angelites of angels and daijels (male angels), and Airlie flew even higher and more to the right to see more of his life in the existence.

As Airlie went flying he came across a galaxy that did not have that much yet. It was only three worlds in it. A yellow world, a low-lit blue world, and a world with nothing on it yet. Just made out of clay with no water to help it grow. No clouds to make water to flow on it. On top of it were nine worlds though. Three at a time, the first larger than the second, and the third the smallest. Each three was as this. "This must be the galaxy of compass. I heard this world killed their master more than once and brutally too and still they live in comfort. Their master must be the most humbled. I will help him in his quest." Airlie flew down to the low-lit blue planet first. There he saw war and love both at the same time. He saw the most wicked entertainment on their televisions too. "How monstrous. If there is people like on their tube in their real life no wonder their master was hurt so many times. The people here have no true direction. Their paradise will be in ruins."

Then a voice came to him in his ears, "Even though I'm not in office it does not mean I do not love my people. You are far from home, are you?"

"Yes, I am! I am from two galaxies away from here."

"Many people tried to help here just like you. I lived here many times. I don't think it'll work."

"Voice in the sky, what year are we in?"

"Fifteen twenty-two, Egypt. It is a very worried place."

"So master of Egypt, I want to help you. As long as it'll take, my oath is born true. We will start from the beginning and work our way to the top. Direct me in this world and I will then direct the world in your favor. I have done this many times before in other worlds, and I see you need the most help. I want to help you become successful. You are the most intelligent here. Now, voice, show me what you know, and I will find your flesh and we will take it from there."

The voice replied, "Yes, I will take you on this oath, for it is in my best entrust."

Airlie then followed the voice to all he needed to see inside of the Egypt and outside of it. Airlie called the voice John, which means Ezeyiah. They went on to helping each other and then other people too. They also had their run-ins with those that were in fear of the two and their forces. And as time never stops the will have a lot of time to help build their world to a better place. Like Airlie did for Toolip he will do for Ezeyiah. Life will soon become better on Egypt. Soon they will be fly away also be living happily ever after.

The End.